The collections of Black Country Living Museum represent the single largest record of material in Britain which exemplifies the particular contribution of the Black Country to the Industrial Revolution. The region was uniquely rich in coal, ironstone, limestone and fireclay. The Staffordshire 'Thick Coal' - a seam 30 feet thick, on average, was the richest in Britain and in some areas outcropped at the surface. Coal had been extracted in South Staffordshire since the middle ages and the area was known for its iron working by the sixteenth century but in the eighteenth century, the exploitation of coal and the other mineral resources was accelerated by the first successful practical application anywhere of steam power and then later in the century by the creation of the densest network of waterways in the country. Together steam power and canals helped create the Black Country and established it as the greatest iron producing district in Britain and one of the greatest in the world.

Elihu Burritt's description of the Black Country is well known – "black by day and red at night" from the fires of blast furnaces, forges and kilns - but his words, quoted overleaf, tell us more about the uniqueness of the region. Firstly, there was the sheer scale of the industrial activity. Victorian Britain had other major industrial centres but none were so extensive. This was a 'country' – a region stretching from Stourbridge in the south to Wolverhampton and Walsall in the north and from the outer edge of Birmingham in the east to Gornal and Sedgley in the west, within sight of the green hills of south Shropshire. Burritt was certain there was nowhere else in the world like the Black Country. It was, quite simply, the first large scale industrial landscape anywhere. Secondly, there was the sense of continuous production, night and day, twenty four/seven. There is something very modern in this description of a place that never went to sleep.

The term the 'Black Country' dates to the 1830s but it is impossible to establish a consensus on its boundaries – except that it is separate and distinct from Birmingham. Many Black Country people hold a greater sense of allegiance to a particular town or locality than to the wider region. Thus the Black Country can be seen as a collection of about 20 towns each with their own specialist industries and each fiercely proud of their own identity. But look wider to the entire region and any discussion of what made the Black Country so distinctive and instantly recognisable comes back to just one word. Landscape.

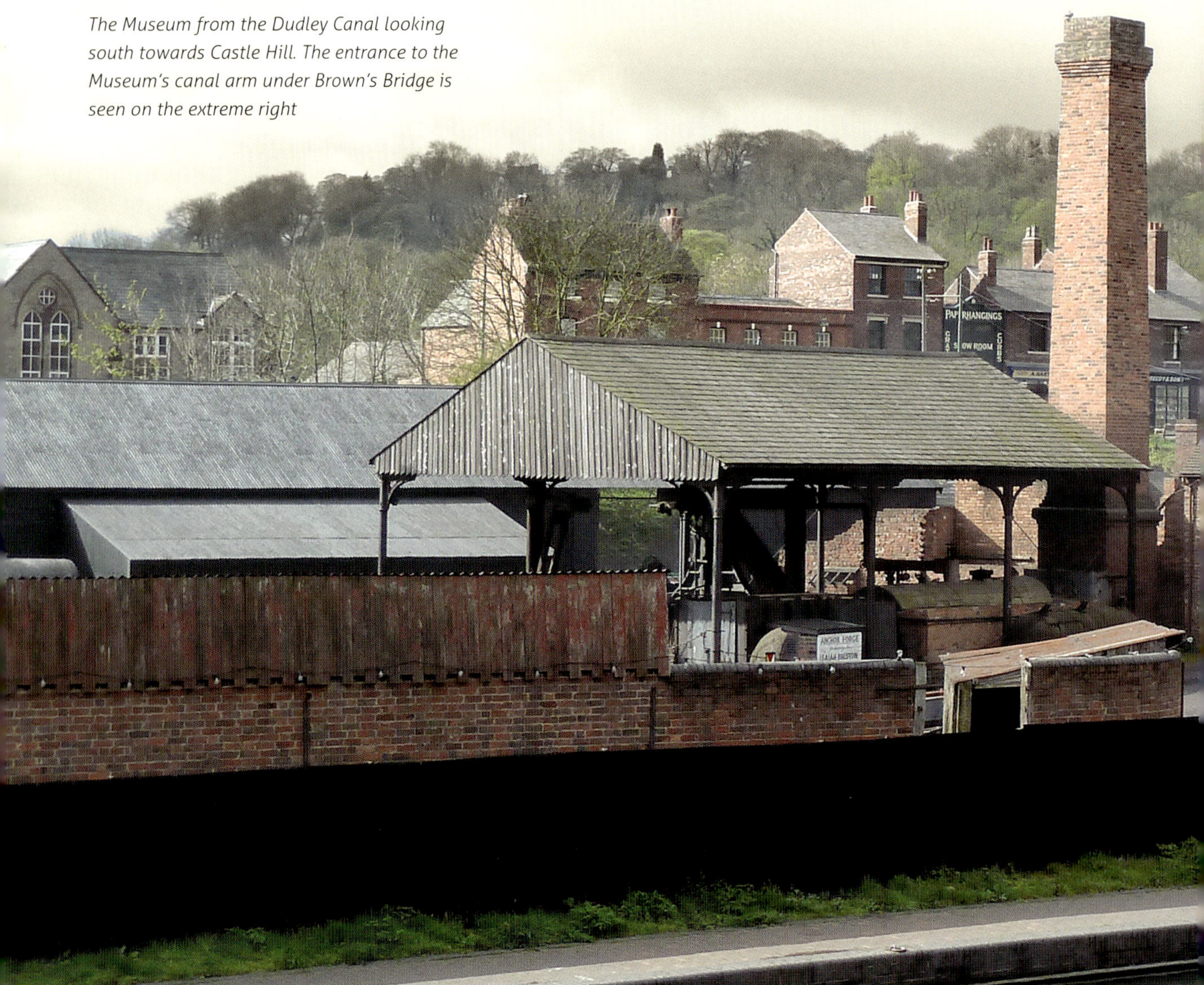

The Museum from the Dudley Canal looking south towards Castle Hill. The entrance to the Museum's canal arm under Brown's Bridge is seen on the extreme right

This was a landscape that had been turned inside out for the extraction of its rich resources: coal, ironstone, limestone and fireclay without sentiment or regard for natural beauty. Vegetation was blighted, trees stunted and burned, grass shrivelled, good farmland neglected and replaced with wide open expanses of colliery waste, piles of slag, cinders and ash. Place names like Daisy Bank, Woodside and Round Oak were throwbacks to a rural past: now there was Quarry Bank, Cinder Bank and Burnt Tree. Disorder and grime predominated. There were stagnant pools of water, quarries of stone, sand and clay pits and even fires of coal slack burning uncontrollably at disused collieries. Visitors were appalled and horrified at such destruction but like Elihu Burritt they marvelled at the extraordinary productivity of the region.

There were roads, mineral railway lines and canals which traversed the land enabling the constant movement of raw materials and finished products to and from the blast furnaces, kilns, rolling mills, foundries, forges and other works. There were chimneys everywhere belching smoke, tall colliery engine houses and pit head frames. The landscape was filled with noise and movement – with the dull thud of heavy forge hammers, the rumbling of rolling mills – the sound of colliery steam engines and colliery pumps – and in small workshops everywhere, the hammering of hot iron on the anvil. And this was a landscape filled with people: colliers - men and boys - foundry and forge workers, covered in smut and with fierce white eyes, boatmen, women chain makers and others who lived out their entire lives in this strange world. From the late eighteenth century, the Black Country acted as a magnet for people looking for work and opportunity. The population exploded and towns like Dudley, West Bromwich and Wolverhampton underwent huge expansion and large parts of the Black Country acquired a solidly urban character.

The range of Black Country industries and products was considerable and it impacted across Britain and the World. In the mid-nineteenth century, the Black Country produced 22% of Britain's total output of iron much of which was converted to the relatively pure and tensile wrought-iron and worked in rolling mills, boiler shops and forges to make a wide range of goods. Nails, chain and anchors, edge tools, locks, anvils, vices, steel traps, tubes, pots and pans brought worldwide fame to towns like West Bromwich, Willenhall and Cradley Heath. Black Country manufacturers supplied the cast-iron pillars and glass of the Crystal Palace built for the Great Exhibition of 1851, made the anchors of some of Britain's most famous ships – Brunel's 'Great Eastern' and the 'Titanic' - and in 1829 supplied the United

States with its first ever steam locomotive, 'The Stourbridge Lion'. There was also leather working, the making of fireclay goods such as drain pipes and sanitaryware, glass and glassware, soap and other chemical based manufactures.

When this first wave of industry peaked and then declined in the later nineteenth century, a second phase of industrial development took over and sustained the industrial predominance and international reputation of the Black Country through the first half of the twentieth century. Steel making, chemical based industries, light engineering including car and motorcycle manufacture and the making of electrical goods became important to the regional economy. Into the 1950s and 1960s the Black Country preserved the physical, economic and social landscape of the earlier part of the century but thereafter the pace of change began to erode the essential character of the region. In 1968 Baggeridge Colliery, the last coal mine on the South Staffordshire Coalfield, closed. As manufacturing dwindled the canals were deserted. Many of the railways closed. The smoke disappeared and houses, factories and workshops were swept away and replaced with a modern urban landscape typified by new housing, trading estates, shopping malls, hotels and fast food outlets.

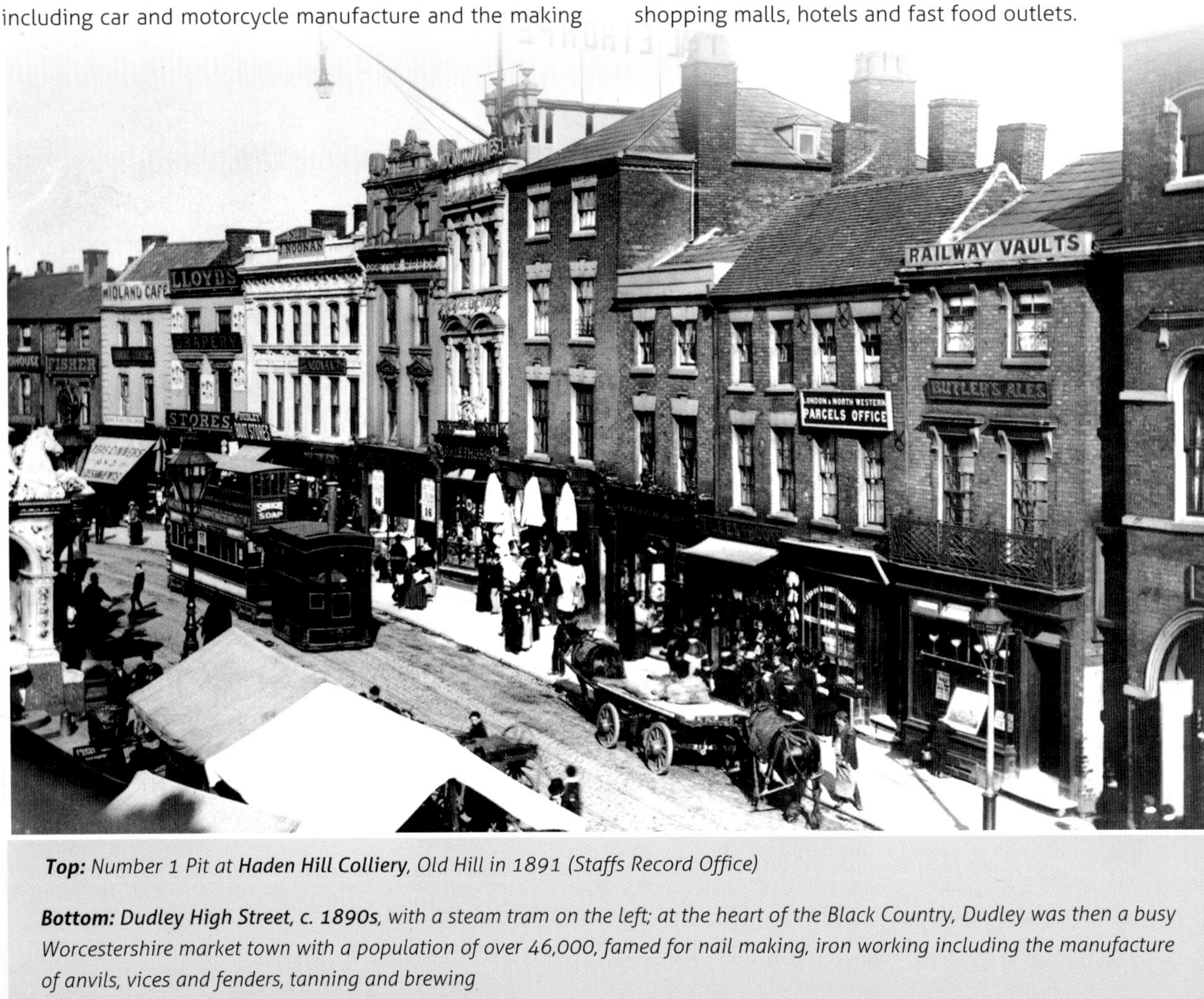

Top: *Number 1 Pit at **Haden Hill Colliery**, Old Hill in 1891 (Staffs Record Office)*

***Bottom: Dudley High Street, c. 1890s**, with a steam tram on the left; at the heart of the Black Country, Dudley was then a busy Worcestershire market town with a population of over 46,000, famed for nail making, iron working including the manufacture of anvils, vices and fenders, tanning and brewing*

It was in this period of rapid change that the idea of a museum dedicated to preserving the traditional Black Country emerged. In 1967 the first exhibition about the Black Country was held in Dudley. It underlined the threat to the region's heritage and attracted considerable community support and with the support of the newly formed Black Country Society the idea of a museum grew. In 1970 further impetus came with the formation of The Friends of the Museum. A site on Tipton Road was secured to create an open air, living museum preserving skills with the buildings and the artefacts demonstrated by costumed demonstrators. The Museum opened on a regular and permanent basis in 1978 and in 2003 acquired the Locksmith's House in Willenhall which preserves in situ an original locksmith's workshop and dwelling house.

The site now comprises 26 acres of former industrial land. On the east it is bounded by the Tipton Road and on the west by the embankment of the former Oxford, Worcester & Wolverhampton Railway – later part of the Great Western Railway – which opened in 1852. The northern edge of the Museum meets the Dudley Canal and looking south is the wooded hill of Dudley Castle and the Zoological Gardens. From 1810-1926, the Museum site was intensively worked for limestone, coal, ironstone and fireclay. A Victorian railway passenger on a train heading north to Wolverhampton would have seen on their right some of the pit head frames of the 40 or 50 shafts which once peppered the site. They could not have failed to notice the large brick chimneys of the limekilns pouring out smoke and the canal arm linking them to the main waterways network. Today, bereft of its chimneys the limekilns form an important part of the site, the canal arm has been cleared and once again is filled with working narrow boats and two of the coal pits have been uncovered.

These original features have now been augmented by some 150 items, including large industrial and public buildings, shops, houses, outbuildings and backyard workshops and many items of street and canal related furniture which have been brought to the site to recreate an authentic Black Country landscape. The site divides into several zones – the Village, the 1930s Old Birmingham Road, the Boat Dock and the Colliery area which is bounded by cottages and a paddock, a reminder that parts of the Black Country retained a semi-rural character. The Museum has also amassed a collection of over 66,000 objects ranging from cars, boats and trams to pots, pans and laundry irons and this collection together with the buildings and structures has been Designated by the Arts Council England as a collection of Outstanding and National Significance.

This Guide features almost 70 key features of the Museum. It explains the origins of each building or structure: many have been carefully rebuilt brick by brick whilst a few are replicas or new builds using old materials to represent typical Black Country structures. This Guide distinguishes between each of these categories. There is also a section on the Locksmith's House in Willenhall. Many of the buildings carry their own stories, of the people that worked and lived in them. This is above all, a living Museum, where visitors can talk with costumed staff, watch demonstrations of traditional Black Country crafts such as nail making, chain making and brass founding, see real coal fires and flaring gas lights and eat fish and chips. In some way, through manufacture or use, virtually everything on view at the Museum proclaims the Black Country and reinforces the identity of the region.

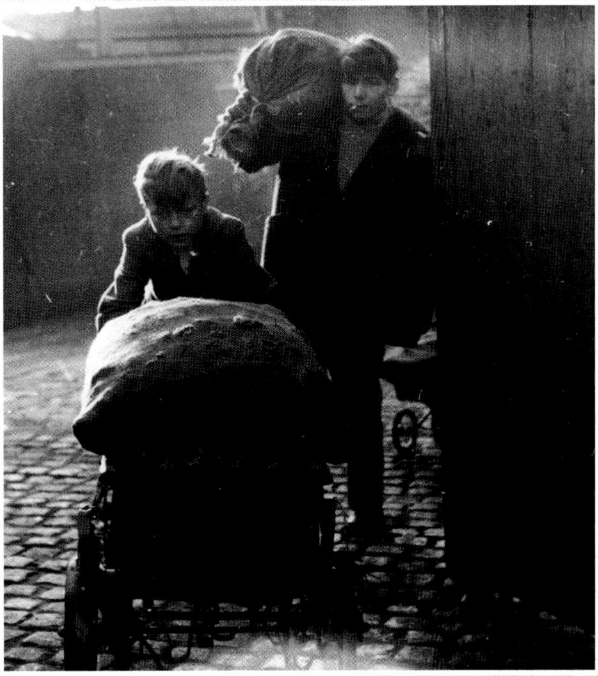

By visiting the Museum it is possible to begin to feel what it was like to live in the Black Country when the region was at the peak of its industrial power. For some, poverty was never far away. Learn about the women chain makers and their struggle in 1910 for a minimum wage and the Pawn Broker's Shop where people would pawn their own bed linen to obtain short term credit. The histories of the houses and cottages tell of levels of poverty, overcrowding and deprivation unimaginable in the twenty first century. These houses can appear quaint today but a hundred years ago some of them had no running water and no flushing toilet. Few had electricity before the 1930s. The Museum, therefore, is more than a purveyor of nostalgia: it aims to engage with audiences in ways that enables history to act as a catalyst so that people can think about their own lives. We want to have a positive, enjoyable and inspiring influence on visitors of all ages and how they contribute in whatever small way to creating a better society and tackling the challenges of the modern world. The story we tell of the Black Country is how 'they' became 'us'.

Above: *Pushing coal home in an old pram, c. 1950*

1 *built:* **1870 & 1888**

Museum Entrance

The Museum entrance is flanked by the brick facades of two Black Country buildings.

On the left of the entrance is the three storey facade of the **Rolfe Street Public Baths,** Smethwick, which was built by the local Board of Health and opened on 7 May 1888. Behind the facade were shed-like structures supported by cast-iron arches which contained two swimming pools, twenty eight slipper baths, two showers and a municipal laundry. The baths were an immediate success providing segregated bathing on different days. Mixed sex bathing was only introduced in 1927.

It was not easy in the nineteenth century for the working classes to keep themselves clean. A shortage of water, a lack of space (and therefore, of privacy) and the expense of baths made it difficult for the average working class family to take a bath. But from 1840s public baths were established through pressure from public health reformers and when construction of the Rolfe Street baths began in 1886, Richard Tangye, a local industrialist and benefactor contributed almost a ninth of the total cost. By 1915 there were 343 public baths in Britain.

To the right of the entrance is the front elevation of the **Old Patent Tube Works** from Smith Road, Wednesbury which is undated but probably built around 1870. Tube making was found in several parts of the Black Country but it was particularly associated with Wednesbury where it was established in 1811 by John Russell. Some locals mistakenly called the premises the 'Anchor Works' because of the company's anchor trade mark which was displayed in the centre of the facade.

***Bottom:** The brick front of the **Old Patent Tube Works** from Wednesbury which now forms part of the entrance complex*

***Top:** Rolfe Street Public Baths: the drawing of the front elevation opposite shows every brick and tile numbered for the reconstruction*

Dominating the Museum Entrance is a 1,500 ton chassis press built in 1913 by Wilkins and Mitchell of Darlaston and used by Rubery Owen until 1970. Established in Darlaston in 1893, Rubery Owen & Co pioneered production engineering techniques in the automotive components industry, building the first independent steel chassis frame for Daimler in 1898 and developing the cold pressing of side sections for commercial vehicles with this press, nicknamed the 'back breaker'.

***'Winston Churchill'**, an 0-6-0 tank engine, built in 1923 by Manning Wardle, Leeds which worked from c.1948-68 at the Shut End Colliery site, Kingswinford*

The Wilkins & Mitchell 1,500 ton chassis press

Automotive Collection

Bradburn & Wedge Motor Garage

The Motor Garage is a modern Museum construction but its front is based on the garage of Bradburn & Wedge, established by William Howard Bradburn (1882-1959) in 1915, in a former horse tram depot in Darlington Street, Wolverhampton.

1931 Sunbeam six cylinder Coupé

In 1918 he was joined by Harry Wedge and although he remained with the business for only four years the firm retained his name to the end. The firm began as motor engineers, coach and body builders but by 1919 were acting as agents for many leading car makers including Austin, Riley and Morris and local manufacturers, Sunbeam. Heavily involved in overhauling military vehicles during the Second World War, the company continued to expand in the 1940s and 1950s providing work for 230 employees. Their Darlington Street premises were rebuilt in 1947 and the Salop Street premises at the rear in 1949-50. The garage was demolished to make way for the Wolverhampton Ring Road.

The Garage contains a display of vehicles from the Museum's collection which provides a unique record of the success enjoyed by Black Country motor manufacturers between 1900 and 1935 although the collection also includes four post-war vehicles, the most recent being a Westfield 'Topaz' coupé of 1986. For a time Wolverhampton and to a lesser extent, Tipton, Dudley and West Bromwich were well-known centres of car making and the vehicles produced by Star, Sunbeam, Bean, Briton, Clyno and AJS enjoyed considerable popularity: all these makes are represented in the collection. Some of the vehicles are extremely rare: the 1903 Sunbeam is one of only four surviving from that year; the 1912 Star 'Victoria' is again one of four surviving from that year and remains in near original condition. The Museum's 1914 Briton is one of only six to survive in the UK and the 1931 AJS is another extremely rare vehicle. Commercial vehicles include a 1925 lorry made by the Dudley based maker, Bean and a 1936 three wheeler tradesman's van by Stevens Brothers of Wolverhampton. The Museum has a unique Guy-Morris fire engine of 1924 with the chassis made by Guy of Wolverhampton. There is also a Model T Ford delivery van of c. 1920 used by Brevitts, carriers of Walsall.

Top: *Featured in the 1931 Sunbeam catalogue was this 16 hp six cylinder Coupé with a sliding roof costing £650.*

Above: *The Star 'Victoria' of 1912 outside the* ***Bradburn & Wedge Garage*** *at the Museum*

Motorcycle Collection

The Museum has a comprehensive collection of early motor cycles including representatives of almost every significant Black Country manufacturer. One of the most famous makers was Sunbeam who were famed for their racing machines in the 1920s as well as their racing cars and aero engines; the collection includes a 1913 Sunbeam which is the earliest known surviving motor cycle by the company. Some of the bikes are extremely rare. A 1927 Sunbeam with its original side car is believed to be unique and the 1921 Orbit is the only complete running example in existence. There are also bikes by AJS, Clyno, Wolf and Rockson. The oldest is a 1912 Clyno Solo and the latest a 1936 Sunbeam.

***Top:* *Bean 14 Tourer of 1925,* built by A. Harper Sons & Bean, Tipton. For a few years in the early 1920s Bean outsold both Austin and Morris**

***Centre:* *Sunbeam* began production of motor bikes in 1912 and this $2\frac{3}{4}$ hp model of 1913 is the earliest known Sunbeam motor bike in existence**

Above: *A factory replica of a 499 cc 3.5 hp Sunbeam T T racing bike of 1921*

The Bus Shed

Bus and Trolley Bus Collection

The Bus Shed was built in 2008 to house buses and trolley buses from the Museum's collection.

As elsewhere in Britain, motor bus services date to the early 1900s when electric tram operations were at their peak. In 1904 the Birmingham & Midland Motor Omnibus Company was founded to operate buses on behalf of the British Electric Traction Company. The company was later better known as Midland Red and grew to be the largest bus operator in Britain after London Transport with services covering most of the Midlands. From 1923 the company took the unusual step of building most of its own buses and this continued until 1970. In Wolverhampton motor buses were first tried in 1905 using three Wolseley double-deck vehicles; West Bromwich started its first bus service in 1914 and Walsall in 1915.

By the 1920s, popular opinion was turning against the tram. With more cars on the road, trams came to be seen as causing unnecessary congestion on busier roads. Increasingly boarding a tram in the middle of the road became more hazardous. Moreover, the operators were faced with the prospect of replacing ageing infrastructure – principally track and overhead systems – and in some cases ageing vehicles. Wolverhampton began to replace its trams in 1923 and chose to invest heavily in trolley buses which had first run in Britain in 1911. Like most electric trams the trolley bus draws its power from an overhead supply but because they have pneumatic rubber tyres like motor buses, they need a second pole and wire to complete the electric circuit. Trolley buses were enormously successful in Wolverhampton and there was considerable expansion of the system up to the late 1930s. Walsall also turned from trams to trolley buses, starting in 1931.

Trolley buses were cheaper to operate than buses and as the driver could steer the vehicle they were better suited to busy town centre streets than trams. Wolverhampton became the second largest trolley bus operator in the country and in 1950 two thirds of its fleet consisted of trolley buses. Wolverhampton was also an important centre for the manufacture of trolley buses: in 1926, Guy Motors started the building of trolley buses with the first ever six wheeled trolley bus and Sunbeam set up a Commercial Vehicles Company in 1931. In 1949 the Sunbeam business was taken over by Guy although the company opted to use the Sunbeam name for all its trolley buses until production ceased in 1962. By the 1960s, the continuation of trolley bus systems in Britain was being questioned on the grounds of cost and they were rapidly closed down. The last trolley bus ran in Wolverhampton in 1967 and in Walsall in 1970.

Representing bus operations in the Black Country, a West Bromwich double-deck bus, Number 174, a Weymann bodied Daimler, one of 20 ordered in 1952 and a Midland Red D9, Number 5342 of 1963 can be seen on display. The Museum also owns a Guy Vixen coach of 1948 which was originally owned by a coach operator in Devon. The trolley bus collection includes two operational trolley buses made by Sunbeam of Wolverhampton: Number 433, a 1946 'W' built for Wolverhampton Corporation which was re-bodied in 1959 by Roe and 862, a 1955 model supplied to Walsall. Awaiting long term restoration is a rare and early Wolverhampton trolleybus, Number 78, made by Guy Motors in 1931; it is one of only two flat 'piano front' style trolley buses surviving.

The open rear platform of Wolverhampton trolley bus 433 allowed for quick boarding and alighting. This bus was used on the last day of trolley bus operations in Wolverhampton on 5 March 1967

Trolley buses last ran in Britain in Bradford in 1972 and the Museum's trolley bus route is currently the longest in the country

Buses and trolley buses from the Museum's collection

Top: *Wolverhampton 433 with a Sunbeam W4 chassis, built 1946 and rebodied by Charles H Roe of Leeds in 1959*

Centre: *Walsall Corporation Trolley Bus, with a Sunbeam F4A chassis, Number 862, built 1955 and withdrawn in 1970*

Bottom: *Midland Red D9, Fleet number 5342 of 1963*

Top: *Sunbeam trolley buses in Walsall on the Bloxwich service, 23 August 1950; below the Corporation Transport clock from Victoria Square, Wolverhampton'*

Bottom: *'Setright Speed' ticket machine, c. 1950s and a West Midlands area bus conductor's badge*

6 built: 1923

Springfield Brewery, Wolverhampton

War Memorial

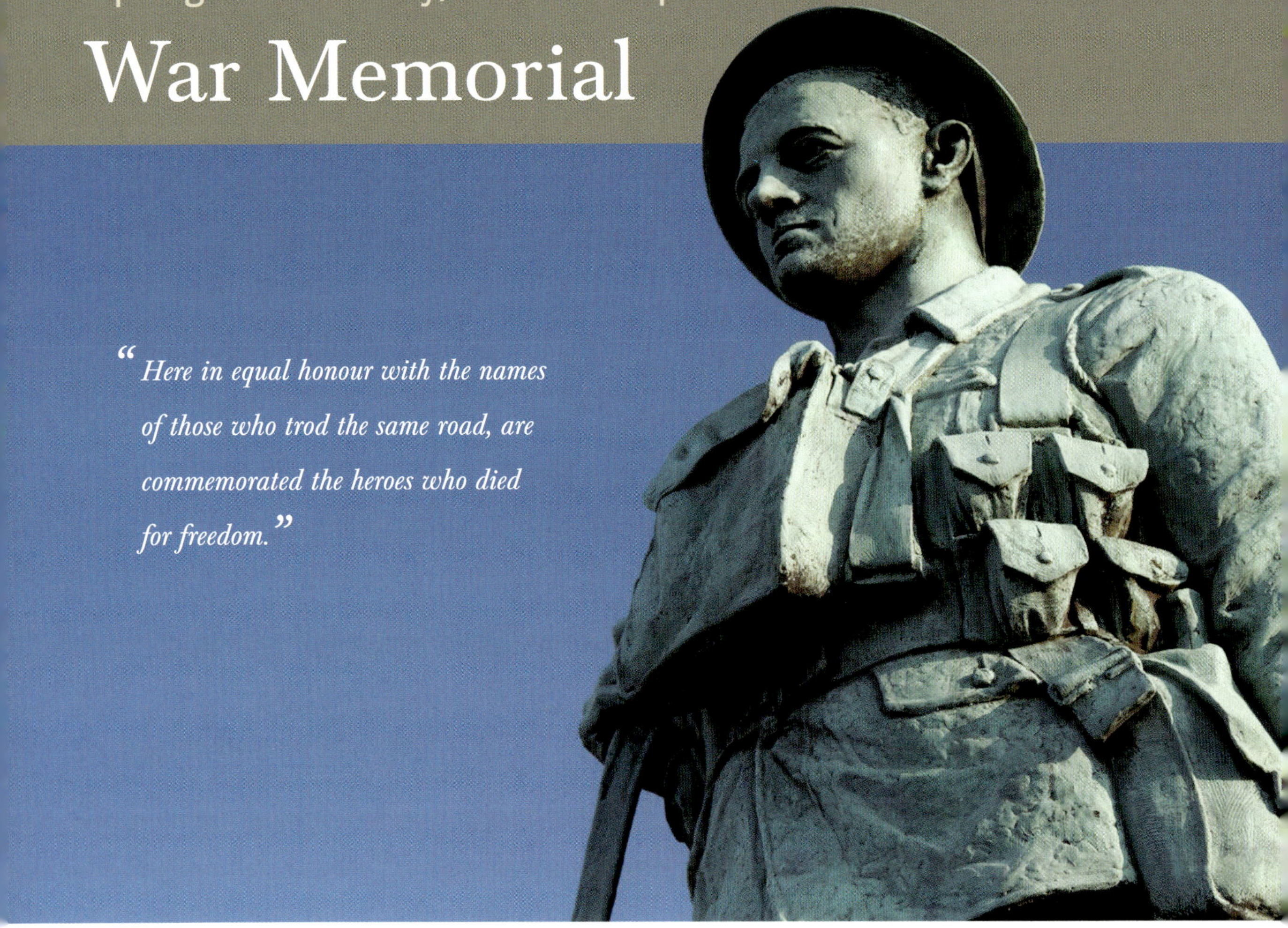

"Here in equal honour with the names of those who trod the same road, are commemorated the heroes who died for freedom."

The War Memorial, consisting of a bronze figure of a British soldier mounted on a granite plinth, was originally erected in 1923 at William Butler's **Springfield Brewery, Wolverhampton** to commemorate not only those who had fallen in the First World War but also those who had served and survived. For many years it stood in the brewery yard close to the entrance. In 1949, the firm added a Second World War roll of honour.

Following several near misses by motor lorries, the monument was moved to a safer spot near the maltings and when these were demolished in 1979 it was moved to the brewery's sports club. When the club closed in 1986 the memorial returned to the brewery but after the closure of the brewery in August 1991, a new home was found at the Territorial Army Centre at Fallings Park, Wolverhampton.

So that the memorial could be seen and appreciated by a wider audience, the War Memorial was moved to the Black Country Living Museum with the assistance of the West Midlands Reserve Forces and Cadets Association in October 2009. A Rededication Service was held in March 2010 and since then, a Remembrance Service attended by the Springfield Brewery Pensioner's Association, and open to all visitors, has become a regular calendar event on 11 November each year.

The bronze figure of the soldier was modelled by Robert Jackson Emerson (1878-1944) who taught at Wolverhampton Municipal School of Art from 1910-1942

7 setting: 1943

Birmingham Road, Dudley

Cast Iron Houses

These two semi-detached council houses were built in Birmingham Road on the Brewery Fields Estate in Dudley in 1925. In response to an acute shortage of housing at the end of the First World War, a Housing Act was passed in 1919 which required local authorities to build new homes.

The new council houses represented a complete break with the past and a totally new approach to working class housing. The houses were designed to provide plenty of fresh air and light with wide frontages, large horizontal windows in place of the traditional vertical sash window and generous sized garden plots. The services were traditional with gas lighting, a coal fired kitchen range and wash copper but all council houses were built with an indoor WC and a fitted bath supplied with running hot and cold water.

Due to a shortage of building materials and labour after the war, experiments were made with various types of non-traditional construction methods. For these two houses, Dudley Council experimented with cast-iron construction using panels, two feet square, bolted together. The panels were made by the Eclipse Foundry in Dudley but the houses were more expensive than those built of brick and only one other pair was built. The houses were occupied until September 1987 when they were declared unfit for habitation. They were rebuilt at the Museum in 1991.

Number 112 is set in 1943 during the Second World War. By this time electricity had been installed in the house replacing the original gas lighting and enabling a radio to be used; a 1940 Bakelite radio sits on the sideboard. By 1943, food, clothing and petrol rationing were in full force and this was the year when the government launched the 'Make Do and Mend' campaign to encourage people to make clothes last longer. The house contains evidence of life on the 'Home Front'. There are black-out curtains in the windows and tape on the glass to prevent it from shattering in the event of a bomb blast. The bath contains a line to mark the five inch limit of water allowed for one bath a week.

A small **Print Shop** has been erected in the garden of Number 114. It was originally located behind a house in Laburnam Road, Bilston from 1936 until its acquisition by the Museum in 1998. Here Robert James carried out 'Letterpress', the art of setting type and printing by hand. For over sixty years he supplied posters, cards and handbills to local shops, churches and societies.

***Bottom:** The Cast Iron Houses from the rear with the Print Shop on the right*

***Top:** The ground floor bathroom of Number 112 with free standing cast-iron bath and WC with high level cistern, the 'Dauntless Cascade' by Thomas Dudley Ltd., Dudley*

9 *setting:* c.1870

Walking down into the thick

The Drift Mine

The Drift Mine lies at the centre of the Museum's Colliery area. It is a modern construction designed to show how coal was mined in the Black Country in the mid-nineteenth century when output in the South Staffordshire Coalfield was near its peak, accounting for 10% of national production.

The coalfield contained measures of coal, ironstone and fireclay of which the most famous was the 'Staffordshire Thick Coal' or 'Ten Yard' seam, named after its average thickness. This was unique in Britain. Nowhere else was a productive seam of such pureness found but this was just one of several seams occurring in the coalfield. The first was the Brooch coal which was a hot, swift burning coal much valued for domestic use. Next came the Thick Coal and if the top seam had become detached from the rest it was called the Flying Reed. The Thick Coal consisted of ten or eleven beds with almost no rock or 'partings' between them and each had its own name, such as Roofs Coal, Stone Coal, Slipper and Sawyer. The Thick was also used for domestic fires but some of the beds were particularly valued for iron smelting and the quality of Black Country iron was attributed to the use of this coal. Below the Ten Yard Seam was the Heathen Coal, another good quality bed which was considered the best for gas manufacture and for coking (coking produces a relatively smokeless fuel used in iron ore smelting). This was followed by the Rubble Coal and the Stinking or Sulphur Coal. These were of poor quality and not usually worked. The lowest measures included the New Mine Coal, Fireclay Coal and Bottom Coal. The ironstone was found some distance below the coal and this was also split into separate seams, each with its own properties and names such as Black or Top Gubbin, Poor Robin and Blue Flats.

The occurrence of these seams and the depth of the coal from the surface varied across the coalfield. In the centre it lay at a depth of 140 yards but northwards the depth decreased until at Bilston the thick coal outcropped at the surface. The earliest workings were surface 'delves' or 'openworks' – where the coal outcropped at the surface. Deeper seams were worked from vertical Bell Pits which were widened out at their base to form a bell shaped cavity. Underground workings were accessed either by a sloping tunnel or by vertical shafts and this replica mine is the former type enabling the visitor to walk safely into the interior. They were called Drift Mines or 'Walking Down' pits in the Black Country.

Whilst Black Country coal quite literally fuelled industrial expansion in the region, it was, nevertheless, won at the cost of great hardship and misery. Coal mining was a hard and dangerous job. In 1850 there were 189 fatalities with most deaths due to shaft accidents and roof falls. The miners were paid for a 'stint' of work by their employers, the 'butty colliers' or 'charter masters' who often manipulated pay and working conditions to maximise their profits.

Today the visitor follows 'Elija Wedge' through the underground passages. He explains how the mines were run and how timber props were used to support the roof and how boys like 'Little Billy' started work aged ten or eleven in the cold and dark, opening the air doors which directed the air around the pit to prevent gas collecting and exploding. The pit pony, 'Sally' is seen with her minder, 'Matthew', whilst the various methods of extracting the coal emphasise the danger of working in the mines. At the pit bottom Elija tells of the accidents which happened in the shafts and explains how 'rattle' chain was used to lift the coal to the surface. The chain was made up of three separate chains held together with wooden pegs and as a result was much safer than a chain made of single links or rope.

10 *setting:* c.1910

Colliery Waste Heap

Bleak and melancholy expanses of colliery waste were found across the region. The rocky waste and clay was known as 'tocky' and the piles of waste as 'pit banks' or 'bonks'. This bank has been reconstructed using 'tocky' from local workings.

11 *setting:* c.1880

Brook Shaft

This shallow pit was worked from 1846-98 to extract the Bottom Coal which was used to fuel the engine boiler of East Castle Limestone Pit.

Brook Shaft and Racecourse Colliery are linked by a two foot gauge tub tramway used to run the tubs to the 'landsale wharf' or the spoil heap.

Opposite top: *Black Country landscape depicted by Harry Eccleston (1923-2010)*

Two scenes from the Museum's Drift Mine

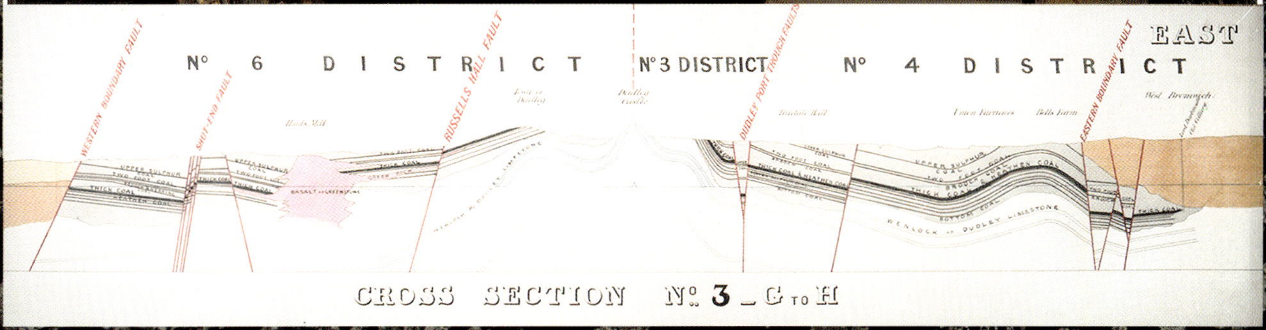

Above: *Female colliery labourers, known as **'Pit Bonk Wenches'** undertook surface work such as sorting and loading coal. These women were photographed at Blue Fly Pit, Burr's Colliery, Hydes Lane, Wednesbury, c. 1890*

Above centre: *A section through the coalfield from east to west centred on Dudley Castle*

Above: *Setting a tall prop or a 'tree' to the roof in the Thick Coal at Lye Cross Colliery, Portway Road, Rowley Regis, c. 1890*

12 setting: c.1910

Racecourse Colliery

The unmistakable outline of the timber pit head frame marks the position of one of the original coal pits on the site. It has been reconstructed as a typical small colliery of c. 1910 and named after the Earl of Dudley's private racecourse which once ran across this part of the Museum before the construction of the railway.

The coal and other minerals on the present day Museum site were owned by the Earls of Dudley and their exploitation was arranged through the Earls' Mineral Agent. The Thick Coal was mined here from 1814-88 whilst the extraction of the lower beds, including the 'Heathen Coal', the 'New Mine Top' and 'Fireclay Coal' continued until 1926. Ironstone was worked on the site in the mid-nineteenth century and fireclay from 1890 to 1912. Limestone was also extracted from the 1840s 35 . Together, the workings of coal, ironstone and fireclay were referred to as East Castle Tipton Pieces and Coneygree. In 1902 the Mine was worked by J & S Baggott and had five underground and two surface workers.

The shaft consists of a circular opening, six feet six inches in diameter lined with brickwork. It was originally 120 feet (37m) deep and has been excavated to a depth of 64 feet. It is surmounted by the pit head frame from which the cage and tub holding the coal were raised and lowered by a rope and pulley usually powered by steam.

The complex of buildings includes a blacksmith's shop, miners' hovel and manager's office in the Weighbridge House rescued from Rolfe Street in Smethwick. The Engine House contains a single cylinder colliery winding engine of c. 1860 used at Amblecote Colliery, near Stourbridge from c. 1910-26. The engine, built by J C Stark & Co of Torquay, is operated regularly and steam is raised in a cross tube vertical boiler made by the Cradley Boiler Company in 1954. There is also a Cappell type fan to aid ventilation underground powered by a small steam engine and several old boilers including an early 'Haystack' boiler of c. 1770.

Above: *Single cylinder colliery winding engine made by J C Stark & Co, Torquay, c. 1860 and used at Amblecote Colliery from 1910-26*

Above: *Gospel Oak Colliery pit and pumping station, Tipton, c.1913*

Top: *Colliers photographed c. 1890 at* ***Blue Fly Pit,*** *Wednesbury*

The World's first working steam engine

Newcomen Engine

In 1712, Thomas Newcomen (1663-1729), from Dartmouth in Devon, invented the world's first successful steam engine in which mechanical work was achieved by a piston moving in a cylinder.

At the time its potential was little realised outside the immediate world of mine owners: it was simply a more effective way of pumping water out of ever deeper coal mines than harnessing animal power. But Newcomen's pioneering work – subsequently refined by James Watt and other engineers – established the steam engine as one of those few inventions which arguably, was to change the course of world history.

The Museum's association with this momentous event is unique and very special. Nothing remains of the original engine but the Museum has built the only full sized working replica which, moreover, is known to have been located in the Black Country. Its exact location is still debated but there is strong evidence to suggest that it was put to work, in 1712, on a coal mine at Coneygree – in Tipton – close to Dudley Castle and no more than a mile or so from the site of the Museum's replica.

The significance of this engine can hardly be overstated. It was a steam engine in name but it did not derive its power from the pressure and expansive force of steam. Instead it used the weight of the atmosphere to push the piston against a partial vacuum in the cylinder, created by condensing steam with cold water. So it has come to be known as an 'atmospheric engine'.

Nevertheless, with its combination of boiler, cylinder, piston and automatic valve gear, the Newcomen engine established all the major components of later steam engines and the development of mechanical power from heat began here with this engine. To people at the time it was a 'Fire Engine' which burned huge quantities of coal and belched thick smoke. It was hugely inefficient but it accelerated industrial growth in South Staffordshire. It helped give the region its name and kept it going 24 hours a day, 'Black by Day - Red by Night' as Elihu Burritt, the United States Consul in Birmingham observed in 1868. Newcomen's pioneering work first made possible the '24/7' regime which propelled industrial growth across the Western World. It freed industrial production from the uncertainties associated with wind and water power, human and animal muscle. And it all started here, so it seems, within view of the ruins of the fourteenth century Dudley Castle.

***Right:** Detail of a drawing of 1725 believed to be of a Newcomen engine installed to pump water at the York Buildings Waterworks Company, London*

14 setting: c.1920

Sedgley Road, Woodsetton

Toll House

Mrs Hodgkiss and her daughter, Lillian, outside Toll House c. 1920

The Toll House was built in 1843. It stood at the Littleworth Gate, Woodsetton on the Sedgley to Tividale Turnpike Road which was authorised by Act of Parliament in 1841.

Turnpike roads were gated roads maintained by trusts empowered by law to impose tolls on travellers. They flourished between c. 1750 – 1850. The tolls were displayed at each toll gate; they varied according to the type of vehicle or goods passing through and were collected by a keeper – usually an employee of the trust – who occupied a specially built toll house.

Like most toll houses this is a single storey structure with a living room containing a kitchen range, two bedrooms and an outhouse with a wash copper, stone sink and baking oven. Two small side windows in the porch provided a good view of the road and below them are built up sections apparently put there to prevent people urinating in the corners. After the middle of the nineteenth century the powers of many turnpike roads were allowed to lapse and tolls ceased to be collected on public roads in Britain in the 1890s. This toll house probably ceased to be used for collecting tolls in the 1870s.

From 1904 to 1927 Ann Hodgkiss moved to the house with four of her nine children following the death of her husband. At a weekly rent of two shillings and sixpence payable to the landlord, the Earl of Dudley, the dwelling offered cheap accommodation. It had no gas or water. An oil lamp was used in the main room and candles in the bedrooms. The family obtained their water from the brook which ran through the garden. The toilet was originally a privy-midden built directly over a cess-pit. The family grew vegetables in the garden and kept a few chickens which were killed when they were past laying.

The period setting is the early 1920s by which time Mrs Hodgkiss was living there with one remaining daughter, Lillian, who for a time worked for Palethorpe's sausage factory in Tipton. She left the house in c. 1924 when she married and Mrs Hodgkiss died in 1927. Members of her family who remembered the house provided detailed descriptions of the interior and garden enabling the Museum to accurately reconstruct it.

*Relocated at the Museum, **Toll House** preserves its road side location flanked each side by well tended gardens*

***Centre:** The interior arrangement of the furnishings is based on recollections provided by the family*

14 setting: c.1920

Cooper's Bank, Gornal Wood

Jerushah (Tilted Cottage)

Buildings leaning together at crazy angles and held together by iron tie rods because they had sunk into old forgotten mine workings were once common across the Black Country. They were called 'pit-pulled' and 'Jerushah', from Cooper's Bank, Gornal Wood on the western fringes of the Black Country, is an example. It was probably built around 1847 when Cooper's Bank consisted of a group of cottages scattered across the small coalmines, quarries and brickworks of the area. In 1881 the cottage was occupied by Benjamin Meredith, a brick layer and from the early 1900s up to 1984 the house was occupied by members of the Bradley family. John Bradley who lived there in the early 1900s was a general labourer.

When the house was first built, water came from a well in the garden which also contained a privy and pig sty. Around 1915 the front elevation was altered. A new front door and larger windows to the living room and bedroom were inserted and at the same time, a brewhouse – or 'brew'us' – was added on the end nearest the road. After John's death the house passed to his sons – first Joseph who lived there with his wife, Seneh until his death in 1939. Joseph worked for a time as a colliery clerk. Following Seneh's death in 1951, the house passed to the younger son, John who lived there with his wife Jerushah. He died in 1960 but Jerushah lived on alone as the last resident of the house until October 1984. The house has been named after her.

In 1986 the house was dismantled and the angle of the tilt carefully replicated at the Museum. The house has been returned to its state around 1915 with a kitchen range fitted in the original large kitchen fireplace whilst the brew'us contains a sink and wash copper for doing the weekly wash and a second range which was used for cooking. Artificial light is provided by paraffin lamps and the red floral wall paper is based on oral testimony. The rose trellis in the front garden is a replica of one in the original garden.

Above: ***Jerushah,*** *its brewhouse and the kitchen range in the main living room*

Jerushah in Cooper's Bank Road, Gornal Wood, c. 1985

16 *setting:* c.1890

Coseley Road, Bilston

Pitt's Cottage

The origins of Pitt's Cottage are uncertain but it is believed to have been built about 1890, possibly by Sam Pitt (c. 1855-1953) who, with his wife, Nancy, is the earliest recorded occupant of the dwelling. The cottage was not the work of a professional builder and showed all the signs of amateur construction with scant foundations and rickety walls made of second-hand bricks.

The cottage was built on a small plot of land, surrounded by privet hedges. The garden contained a pig sty and an earth closet constructed of corrugated iron which was regularly emptied by night soil men. The cottage originally consisted of just two rooms although there is evidence of a second bedroom, reached through the first, of timber construction.

Above: *The pail closet, widely adopted in poorer homes from the 1860s contained a bucket under the fixed wooden seat to collect the waste. As this was emptied regularly it prevented large accumulations of raw sewage under the seat*

Sam and Nancy would have needed a second bedroom as they had eight children. The house lay at the foot of a railway embankment carrying the Bilston branch of the Great Western Railway. Beyond the railway line were the Bilston sandstone quarries where Sam Pitt worked before finding employment at the Caponfield Ironworks across the road from the cottage. All around there were disused coal shafts and low waste heaps, short rows of terraced housing, allotments, more railway lines and canal wharfs and basins connecting with the Birmingham Canal.

The family tradition is that Sam Pitt was inclined to drunkness and was eventually thrown out by Harry, one of his five sons, who then lived there with his wife Sally. In about 1950 he bricked up the front entrance and rebuilt and enlarged the back kitchen. The facilities inside the cottage were basic. The kitchen contained a cast-iron range with an oven; light was obtained by a paraffin lamp hanging from the ceiling. There was no water, only an outside tap by the garden gate. The cottage interior is remembered as being gloomy containing a Singer sewing machine and an old clock face on the wall. After Harry's death, Sally lived there alone until she died early in 1969. The cottage then fell derelict until 1988 when the cottage was dismantled brick by brick by the Museum.

Top right: *the derelict cottage in c. 1985 and main picture, relocated at the Museum*

17 *setting:* c.1937

The Ross, Blackheath

Lench's Oliver Shop

Lench's Oliver shop was built between 1908 and 1910 by Onan Lowe, an oddworker. Oddwork is a Black Country term for the making of miscellaneous small items of wrought-iron by hand. It was situated behind a row of houses on the Ross, Blackheath and accessed by a cart entry in the row.

It takes its name from the 'oliver', a spring loaded hammer operated by a treadle which allowed the blacksmith to guide or manipulate the metal being forged with both his hands as he worked. The tension came from an overhead ash pole (or a large metal spring) and these ensured the hammer heads returned to the upright position.

The workshop originally had ten forges and each had its own chimney built by laying one brick on edge on two opposite sides and two bricks on edge on the other giving a distinctive overhanging at the corners. Chimney stacks of this construction were once common in the Black Country; this may have been to give them more stability if the lime mortar holding the brickwork failed. Only the windows of the warehouse and office at the end of the building are glazed; the windows in the workshop are simply shuttered to provide ventilation and the doors are of stable construction so the upper half could be hooked back and opened.

On the other side of Ross was The Excelsior Works of William Thomas Lench, a large nut and bolt concern, established in 1880. In 1937 T W Lench purchased Lowe's Shop and used six of the ten hearths to make hooks, shackles, clips and other fastenings of wrought-iron. An electric motor was installed in the timber shed at the opposite end to the warehouse, once used by Lowe for storing stock, to power the air supply to the hearths via line shafting. Demand for oddwork gradually declined after 1945 but even as late as 1979 there were three oliver smiths at work. In 1983 the firm of T W Lench donated the workshop and its contents to the Museum. Before the building was taken down a thorough record was made of all the material in the workshop. Once the full brick by brick reconstruction was completed the relevant material was put back exactly where it had come from.

18 The Paddock

In between the factories, foundries and forges were patches of grazing land, small fields and allotments which served as a reminder of the rural character of the region. The Museum's horses graze here. The Black Country was notoriously untidy and it was common to see old equipment lying disused and neglected, like the large wrought-iron egg-end boiler which rests in the field opposite Lench's Oliver Shop.

Top: *Advertisement of 1936 for Lench's 'Admiralty Brand' bolts: the firm was an approved supplier to the Admiralty from 1892*

Above: *Lench's recorded in c. 1983 before the take down*

20 *setting:* 1930s

The Fairground

The Fairground represents a typical 1930s travelling fair. These were owned by a fairground family or group of families who would tour the country setting up for a week on waste ground. This particular fair is owned and operated by the Jones family of Cradley Heath who started travelling with fairs in the early 1880s.

Most of the rides including the Shooting Gallery, Swing Boats and Helter Skelter (which is also known as a 'Slip') date to the 1930s. The Ark Speedway was built by Lakin of Streatham, London, in 1932 for the Townsend family and it originally travelled around the south of England. The Brooklyn Cakewalk is an almost forgotten ride imported from America. This one was rescued from a scrap yard in the north of England. The Juvenile (kid's ride) has all its original running gear and like all the fairground equipment has been carefully restored in a traditional style.

The Empire Arcadia is a typical amusement arcade of the 1930s and the Hook a Duck is a 1930s hoopla stall aimed to provide a 'prize every time' for younger children. The Coconut Shy dates to c. 1900 and the Striker to the 1800s.

Top: *Slides built in a spiral around a high tower resembling a light house first appeared in British fairgrounds around 1900;* ***'helter skelter'*** *is an old term for disorderly haste*

Above: *The fairground lit against a night sky at one of the Museum's evening events with from left, the* ***Ark Speedway****, the* ***'Kid's Ride'*** *and the* ***Rifle Range***

21 *setting:* **1930s**

Fighting Cocks, Wolverhampton *(replica)*

The Conway Garage

Alec Broome (1903-87)

This building is a replica built of modern materials representing the Conway Garage which formerly stood near the 'Fighting Cocks' on the Wolverhampton to Dudley Road. It belonged to Alexander 'Alec' Broome (1903-87) who achieved fame as a motor mechanic working for the Sunbeam Motor Company of Wolverhampton.

Alec Broome was apprenticed to The Sunbeam Motor Company in 1919. He was soon transferred to the company's experimental and racing team in the 1920's and was involved in the company's development of cars which could challenge the land speed record and were capable of competing in Grand Prix races throughout Europe and events at the Brooklands Circuit in Surrey. He also worked with the land speed record breaker, Sir Malcolm Campbell (1885-1948) on several occasions. When Sunbeam car production ended in 1935 he opened this garage the following year.

The building was a proprietary timber and asbestos shed purchased for £350 and located in front of the bungalow he occupied with his wife. The garage was typical of small suburban and country garages of the time which thrived on sales of petrol and providing a 'make do and mend' service at a time when the life of car engines, brakes and tyres was limited and new cars expensive and in short supply.

The garage is set in the 1930s and houses vehicles from the Museum's collections. Pride of place goes to Alec Broome's own 1932 Sunbeam 16 H P Sportsman's fixed coupé in all-black. He purchased this in the 1950s and when it was retired in the mid-1960s, it was placed at the workshop end of the garage where it was kept in immaculate condition and admired by all who called.

***Above:** The Museum's **Star Comet 18** of 1931, made by the Star Motor Company of Bushbury, Wolverhampton standing on the forecourt of the Conway Garage*

22 setting: 1920s

The Albion Depot & Tram Collection

The Albion Tram Depot is located alongside the current northern terminus of the Museum's Tramway. This has been built to the three feet six inches narrow gauge which was a distinctive feature of the tram systems of Birmingham and the Black Country. The depot is a partial rebuild of a tram depot from Handsworth, near the ground of West Bromwich Albion Football Club – hence the name – and is believed to have been built in the 1880s to house steam trams of the South Staffordshire Tramways Company.

The first tramway in the Black Country was inaugurated in Wolverhampton in 1878. The trams were horse drawn and ran on standard gauge track (four feet eight and a half inches). A fleet of steam trams operated by the South Staffordshire & Birmingham District Steam Tramways Company commenced service in 1883. The narrow gauge lines of this company connected several towns in the Black Country including West Bromwich, Wednesbury, Walsall and Bloxwich, Dudley and Darlaston. In 1893, the company – now renamed the South Staffordshire Tramways Company – introduced electric trams between Walsall and Pleck. From 1884 steam trams, operated by the Dudley and Stourbridge Steam Tramways Company, ran between Dudley and Stourbridge. In 1898 this company was taken over by the British Electric Traction Company and they replaced steam with electric trams on this route in 1899. The company also provided an electric tram service to Cradley Heath, Lye, Kingswinford and Blackheath. In 1902 the company took over the Kinver Light Railway which ran between Amblecote and Kinver.

In Wolverhampton, the tramways were taken over by the Corporation in 1900 and narrow gauge electric trams introduced in 1902. Given the opposition to the use of overhead cables, Wolverhampton Corporation adopted the Lorain pick-up system in which electric current reached the tram's motor via a skate, placed beneath the tram, making contact with studs on the surface of the road between the running rails. The tramway operators created a region wide network of cheap and effective public road transport but from the 1920s trams fell from favour across the country. Wolverhampton completed the replacement of its trams with buses and trolley buses in 1928. Two years later, the Dudley and Stourbridge tram service ceased operation and trams were finally abandoned in Walsall in 1933. Birmingham Corporation continued to run trams to Dudley until 1939.

The Museum's Depot provides accommodation for a standard gauge double deck horse tram from Wolverhampton – Car Number 23 – of 1892 built by the Falcon Company of Loughborough and the three narrow gauge electric trams which are used on the regular service. The earliest is Wolverhampton Car 49, an open topped double deck tram built in Preston in 1909. This tram was originally fitted with the Lorain system of ground level electric supply but later converted to a covered top tram with the more conventional overhead system. The other two are single deck trams built by the British Electric Traction Company at their Tividale works between Dudley and Oldbury. Number 5 was built in 1920 and operated by the Dudley, Stourbridge and District Company from their Hart's Hill Depot whilst tram 34 was built in 1919 and operated by the Wolverhampton District Company from their Bilston Depot.

Interior of Wolverhampton Tram 49, built by the United Electric Car Company, Preston, in 1909

Two Birmingham Corporation trams at the Dudley Terminus, Castle Hill, opposite the railway station, c. 1930s

Above: *Wolverhampton* ***Car 49*** *of 1909 which has been restored with an overhead tram pole although it only ever ran in this form with an enclosed upper deck*

Centre: *Wolverhampton horse tram,* ***Number 23****, built at the Falcon Works, Loughborough, 1892 and withdrawn in 1904 when electric trams were introduced by Wolverhampton Corporation*

Above: *Dudley & Stourbridge tram,* ***Number 34****, built at Tividale in 1919*

Salop Street, Eve Hill, Dudley

St. James's School

Before the advent of a national system of education in the 1870s, much of the impetus for educating children came from religious organisations. In 1811 the Church of England established the National Society for Promoting the Education of the Poor in the Principles of the Established Church with the aim of setting up a Church of England School close to every parish church. Four 'National' Schools were set up by the Society in Dudley and one of these was St James's School on Salop Street, Eve Hill, built in 1842, just two years after the building of St James's Church at Eve Hill.

Built of locally quarried Gornal stone, the school was designed by the Dudley architect, William Bourne (c. 1811-70) who also designed the neighbouring church. It originally had leaded lancet windows and stone crosses on the roof and was divided into two separate schools for boys and girls. It was intended there should be a strong emphasis on religious instruction but the school struggled with inadequate funding and poor standards of teaching. In 1868 it became a mixed school for boys, girls and infants.

Growing concern for standards of education and literacy throughout the country led to the passing of the 1870 Elementary Education Act. Locally elected School Boards were required to build new schools and given powers to make school attendance compulsory. The first School Board for Dudley met in 1871 and enforced school attendance for children aged between five and 13 years. At this time, St James's School suffered from inadequate heating and ventilation and in 1904 was recommended for closure following an inspection when it was described as 'dingy, dilapidated and dirty'. Dudley Education Committee was reluctant to close the school and in 1906 the Mixed School was transferred away and continued as a school for infants only.

In 1912 alterations were carried out including the replacement of the front lancet windows with large rectangular ones and provision of new toilets. There was electric lighting by this time. The school underwent a radical modernisation in 1936 when the main building was divided into three classrooms with a central corridor, a new entrance and new cloakrooms. The building closed as a school in 1980 and became a community centre. It finally closed in 1989 when it was declared structurally unsafe. It has been rebuilt to its condition between the alterations of 1912 and 1935 and set in 1912.

***Top:** St James's School in the 1980s when it was a community centre*

***Above:** A class at St James's School in 1925*

Medal struck in 1843 to raise funds to complete the school

The Black Country in the 1930s - *building from* Hall Street, Dudley

Hobbs & Sons Fish & Chip Shop

The building housing Hobbs' Fish and Chip shop and Morrall's Menswear Shop comes from Hall Street, Dudley. It dates to the late 1700s but was refaced with bright red pressed brickwork in 1889. In the early 1900s the shop served as a commercial laundry with Joseph Hobbs establishing his chip shop around 1916.

The origins of fish and chips are uncertain although it is believed that two separate trades – the sale of fried fish and cooked potatoes – were brought together in the 1860s. By the late nineteenth century, fish and chips was widely established as a working class food across industrial Britain.

The impressive tiled interior of the chip shop features hand painted tiled wall panels made by Pilkington's Tile & Pottery Company, Manchester, which have carefully been restored. Joe Hobbs is remembered as being a hard task master and fastidious about the cleaning of the shop interior. He also took particular care in the purchase of his fish which came ashore at Aberdeen and was sent to Birmingham Market. Later Joe had the fish dropped off at Dudley Port Station which was more convenient. He was similarly particular about his choice of flour using a special saffron flour obtained locally which gave the batter a reddish tint.

The involvement of the Hobbs family ended in 1976 when Joe's daughter, Joyce (born 1916) retired. The shop then continued as a Greek kebab shop until 2000 after which it remained unoccupied and derelict until the Museum commenced dismantling the structure in 2006. The shop has been restored with a frying range probably dating to the early 1950s of a design patented in 1932 and made by E W Proctor of Huddersfield, Yorkshire; it was rescued from a fish and chip shop in Scunthorpe. The dining room – or saloon – is lined with wooden benches – some original and some replicas – and has a typical thirties style tiled fireplace.

In the 1930s many of Joseph Hobbs's customers worked in nearby factories or shops. Today visitors can eat their fish and chips in the reconstructed saloon set in 1935.

Top: *Hobbs' fish and chip shop in Hall Street c. 2005*

Bottom: *The reconstructed shop exterior and one of the decorative tiled panels*

The Black Country in the 1930s

Old Birmingham Road

buildings from
Birmingham Street, Oldbury & Hall Street, Dudley

25 H. Morrall's Gentlemen's Outfitters *building from* Hall Street, Dudley

Harry Morrall's Menswear Shop was located next door to Hobb's fish restaurant at 42 Hall Street, Dudley from c. 1928 until 1935. From 1935, the shop was run as a tailors and gentlemen's outfitters by Archibald Victor Rogers. He remained there until his death in 1952 and the following year the shop was taken over by Arthur Ashmore. Harry Morrall lived over the shop with his family from 1928 to 1935. When Mr and Mrs Ashmore moved into the premises in 1954, there was still no bathroom or water upstairs.

Little is known of the detail of Morrall's business. It is likely that he provided every article of clothing apart from suits which were probably made to order by larger garment factories: there were two such factories in Dudley in the 1930s.

The shop is set in 1935 and has been furnished with counters and shelving from E. Minnett's ladies outfitters of Walsall Street, Wednesbury. The stock of Morrall's would have been very similar to the stock which visitors can see today. The shop front display – including the front door window – is based on the one known photograph of Morrall's which shows the shop front crammed with stock following the then current philosophy of 'show more, sell more'. Visitors can buy souvenir 1930s style ties, scarves, gloves and hats in the shop.

26 Humphrey Brothers Builders' Merchants

These four shops were formerly Numbers 12, 14, 16 and 18 Birmingham Street, Oldbury and in 2005 the Museum arranged the transfer of the derelict block dating to c.1850 - 75 to form part of the 'Old Birmingham Road' which is set in the 1930s. The Museum undertook its well practised technique of taking down the buildings brick by brick, numbering each one in the process, to ensure an authentic reconstruction. Little of the interiors survived and so the Museum carried out research to build up a picture of how the shops might have looked in the lead up to the Second World War.

Humphrey Brothers, Builders and Decorators, were at 12 Birmingham Street from 1921 until about 1960 although at one time they also occupied 14 and 16. The shop front is based on its known appearance in the early 1930s when it was dominated by the impressive and ornate green painted timber facia over the goods entrance. Humphreys sold fireplaces, toilets and a wide range of building supplies including 'Walpamur', a flat paint used for internal walls.

The shop window display is dominated by a large fireplace surround of mottled brown and beige tiles and dark oak – typical of the mid-1930s. Inside the shop, the green wash basin and WC with its low level cistern, represents the latest in thirties fashion, coloured bathroom suites having been introduced to Britain from America in 1927.

***Humphrey Brothers** in Birmingham Street, Oldbury, in the early 1930s*

25

Right Top: *The interior of Morrall's*
Right Centre: *Motor bikes on display in Hartill's*
Right Bottom: *Art deco bathroom fittings and 'Walpamur' paint tins in Humphrey Brothers*

27 A. Hartill Motorcycles

In the 1930s, Number 14 was occupied by Humphrey Brothers but the premises have been used to reconstruct a typical thirties motorcycle shop based on A Hartill & Sons of Mount Pleasant, Bilston, another double fronted shop which opened in 1937. Motor cycle manufacture in the Black Country started in the early 1900s but was at its peak in the 1920s and 1930s when a motor cycle could be run for about the third of the cost of a car. Local dealers provided a comprehensive service of sales of new and second hand machines, servicing and the sale of spare parts.

The shop window contains a display of six motorcycles dating to 1929-34 representing three leading Wolverhampton makers of the inter-war years – AJS, Stevens and Sunbeam. The shop contains motor cycle and bicycle accessories and reproductions of advertising material from the 1930s. Some large dealers employed racing riders in sales, to attract enthusiasts and encourage business. The framed photographs on the walls show local riders in action at the Isle of Man Tourist Trophy (T.T.) Races in the 1920s.

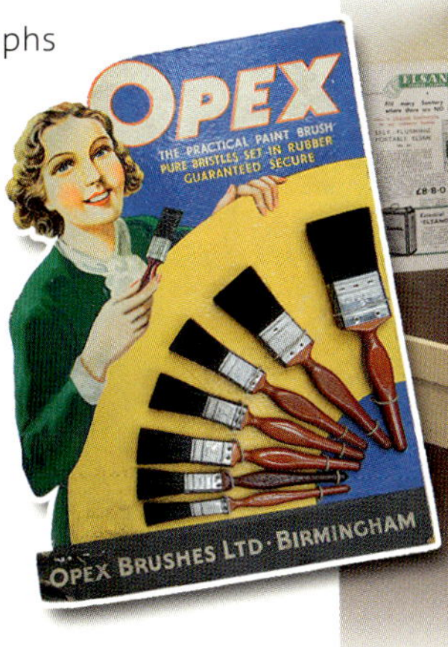

setting: c.1935-39

The Black Country in the 1930s

Old Birmingham Road

Preedy's shop in Cannock, c. 1930s

28 A. Preedy & Sons Tobacconists

Number 16 was occupied by two small independent tobacconists up to about 1932 but the premises are presented here as one of the branches of Alfred Preedy & Sons - well known wholesale and retail tobacconists in the West Midlands - established in Dudley in 1868. By the 1930s they were established as major wholesalers as well as retailers with their own brands of tobacco such as 'Rowley Rag' and stores across the West Midlands.

The front name board is based on Preedy's shop in Cannock and the shop window display represents a typical thirties tobacconist's shop, crowded with brands of pipe tobacco, cigarettes and accessories such as pipes and matches. By the 1930s the briar pipe had replaced the traditional clay tobacco pipe but it is the various brands of cigarette that dominate: between 1914 and 1939, annual tobacco consumption per head almost doubled. This was the age of the cigarette when the health hazards of smoking went largely unchallenged and a tobacconist's shop was a part of every high street.

29 Gripton's Radio Stores (*setting:* 1939)

There was a butcher's shop in Number 18 in the late 1930s. James Gripton's Radio Shop was at Number 4 from the early 1920s until the late 1940s and this reconstruction, set in 1939, contains 'new' and second hand radios for sale, some of which date to the 1920s. The shop undertook repairs in a back workshop which is accessible to visitors through the rear entrance.

Radio shops were a new phenomenon of the era: the spread of mains electricity and technical improvements in radio design encouraged a rapid rise in radio ownership in the 1930s. When the Prime Minister, Neville Chamberlain, announced that Britain was at war with Germany on the BBC on 3 September 1939, there were nearly nine million licence holders in Britain.

30 1930s Domestic Rooms

The brick tunnel and cart entrance provide access to a late thirties kitchen at the rear of Preedy's. The kitchen is unfitted with a free standing kitchen cabinet, table and fireclay sink with a wooden drain board but contains an up to date electric cooker made by the Revo Electric Co. Ltd, Tipton. Upstairs, the front room is set out as a drawing room with original 'Modern Style' wall paper of c.1935 and a three piece suite of oak furniture; the back room is a simple bedroom. Walk through into Number 18 and the front room is furnished as an everyday living room, the back room contains a second bedroom. The stairs lead into a radio repair workshop at the rear of Gripton's shop.

*The late 1930s kitchen **behind Preedy's** with a lightweight aluminium tea kettle on the Revo electric cooker; Revo were well known for their electric street lights but by 1934 were also manufacturing electric cookers*

*The Dining Room **above Gripton's Radio Shop** with oak furniture of the 1920s and 1930s and original 1930s wall paper*

*The interior of **Preedy's** packed with 1930s stock and advertising material*

***Gripton's** contains a representative selection of radios dating from the 1920s and 1930s*

31 setting: c.1900

Millfield Road, Bilston

The Builder's Yard & Office

The Builder's Yard consists of two buildings: the office and a hovel. The stone hovel was originally part of a yard on Millfield Road, Bilston and was built onto a brick office dating from about 1850 or 1860. The original stone hovel has been rebuilt at the Museum but the Office is a replica.

In the yard there is a selection of builder's supplies, including timber, bricks, slates, drain pipes and water closets and chimney pots. The slate came from North Wales but many of the items are of local manufacture. The pile of bricks made by the Ketley Brick Company, Brierley Hill, are a reminder of the former importance of brick making in the Black Country. Chimney pots, ridge tiles and roof finials were made in the region by firms such as Hinton, Perry & Davenhill of Pensnett and Henry Doulton of Lambeth extended their manufacture of sanitaryware to the Black Country when they opened fireclay works at Rowley Regis in 1897. Cast-iron goods, such as WC cisterns, rain water pipes, wash coppers, firegrates, stoves and ranges and grids and grills of every description were made by many of the iron foundries of the region.

32 setting: 1928

The Stonefield Pigeon Loft

originally from Prosser Street, Bilston

The Stonefield Pigeon Loft belonged to Charlie Purslow (1906-98) who worked at the Cannon Iron Foundry, Darkhouse Lane, Bilston as an iron moulder and subsequently for Stewarts & Lloyd's steel works.

The loft stood on ground in Prosser Street, Bilston. It is believed to have been built in 1928 although it may have been erected as early as 1924. It was built by Roger Rickwood who also worked at the Cannon Foundry as a pattern maker. The loft was always painted every year – the brick support pillars or 'stilts' and steps were lime washed – and the outside painted in black and white stripes. The name of the loft was sign written on the side.

Pigeon keeping was a popular pastime in the Black Country, not only for the sport of pigeon racing but also as a source of extra meat and eggs. Charlie Purslow's interest in pigeon racing started when he was a boy and he became a celebrity in pigeon flying circles in Bilston, winning many major prizes over a 70 year period. He was also a member of the national pigeon service during the Second World War when birds were used to take messages into occupied territory. He usually at any time had about thirty birds. He was never one for keeping birds that were not good racers and used to say "they've got to fly or flit". He used to breed the birds every year and knew all his birds by their names. His favourites were always those which had won the greatest number of races: two being "Peggy" and "Bilston Blue". He would often take his tea up to the loft and wait all day for the birds to return.

Top: *The office counter in the Builder's Yard*

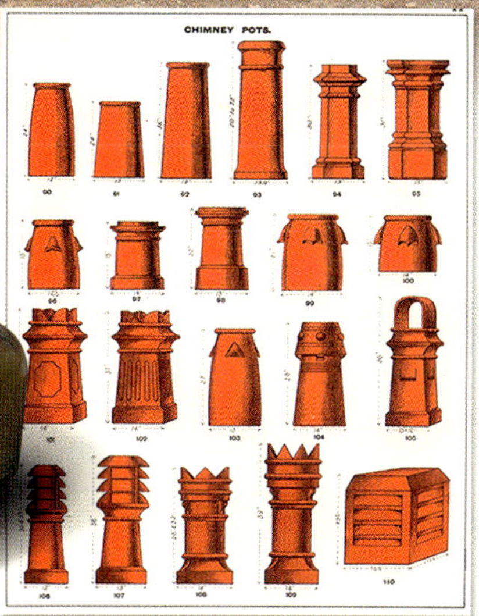

From top: the Gornal stone gable end of the Builder's Yard Hovel; Fireclay water closet; page from the catalogue of Hinton, Perry & Davenhill, Pensnett, West Midlands, c. 1925

Above: The Stonefield Pigeon Loft

Bottom left: 'Mr Bateman's Pigeons' water colour drawing by Harry Eccelstone (1923-2010)

33 *setting:* **c.1935**

Lower High Street, Cradley Heath

The Workers' Institute

The Cradley Heath Workers' Institute stands as a monument to the struggle of the women chain makers of Cradley Heath who laid down their tools in 1910 to strike for a living wage, focussing international attention on the plight of Britain's low paid workers and establishing the principle of a minimum wage.

Growing awareness of the terrible conditions endured in the sweated trades where people – many of them women and children – worked extremely long hours for poverty wages resulted in the passing of the Trade Boards Act in 1909 to establish regulatory Boards and minimum rates in four low paid trades, one of which was the making of hammered chain in small workshops and domestic forges. Women would typically work 13 hour days to earn five shillings a week. When the employers tried to find ways of avoiding paying the new rates and even recalled the iron rods which had already been delivered, the National Federation of Women Workers led by the charismatic Mary Macarthur (1880-1921), called out on strike all those who were working for less than the minimum rate. And so the women laid down their hammers.

Mary Macarthur waged an effective campaign and the striking women won widespread national support. Donations came pouring in and by 22 October 1910 when the strike ended all the employers had agreed to pay the new higher rates. The women's victory was to have a huge impact right across the British Labour Movement. Soon more regulatory Boards were established in other industries as the government accepted for the first time that every worker was entitled to a living wage.

When the strike was won there was a surplus of £1,500 in the fund. Mary Macarthur proposed that it should be used to build a 'centre of social and industrial activity' in the district and a site was chosen on the corner of Whitehall Road and Lomey Town Road (now Lower High Street), Cradley Heath on a spoil heap which had been the venue for many rallies during the strike. The two storey building was designed by Albert Thomas Butler (1872-1952), a local architect, in the Arts & Crafts style. With its prominent gables, leaded windows and tiled panel bearing its name, the building embodies the spirit of traditional 'vernacular' construction and craftsmanship. Thousands of people

Top: *The steeply pitched roof of the* ***Workers' Institute*** *with its double pitched central section is seen to perfection in this view at the Museum with Folke's Park in the foreground*

Top of opposite page: *Mary Macarthur addresses a meeting in Cradley Heath during the strike of 1910.*

attended the opening of the building by the Countess of Dudley on 10 June 1912. The Institute became a centre for educational meetings, social gatherings and trade union activities in Cradley Heath. Between 1915 and 1933, its auditorium operated as a picture house being known locally as 'The Stute'.

In 2004 the building was threatened with demolition because of a planned by-pass and so the Black Country Living Museum was approached to save the building. In 2006 the Heritage Lottery Fund grant aided the reconstruction. The take down enabled the original interior layout which had been obscured by later alterations to be reinstated. Now the building contains reconstructed offices, a news room which tells the story of the 1910 strike whilst the auditorium now serves as a café.

***Centre Right:** Two of the ground floor offices which are set in 1935 and underneath the tiled name panel on the front elevation of the building*

***Above:** the Institute photographed in May 2004 at its original location in Cradley Heath before dismantling*

34 built: 1842

Original features of the Museum site

The Limekilns

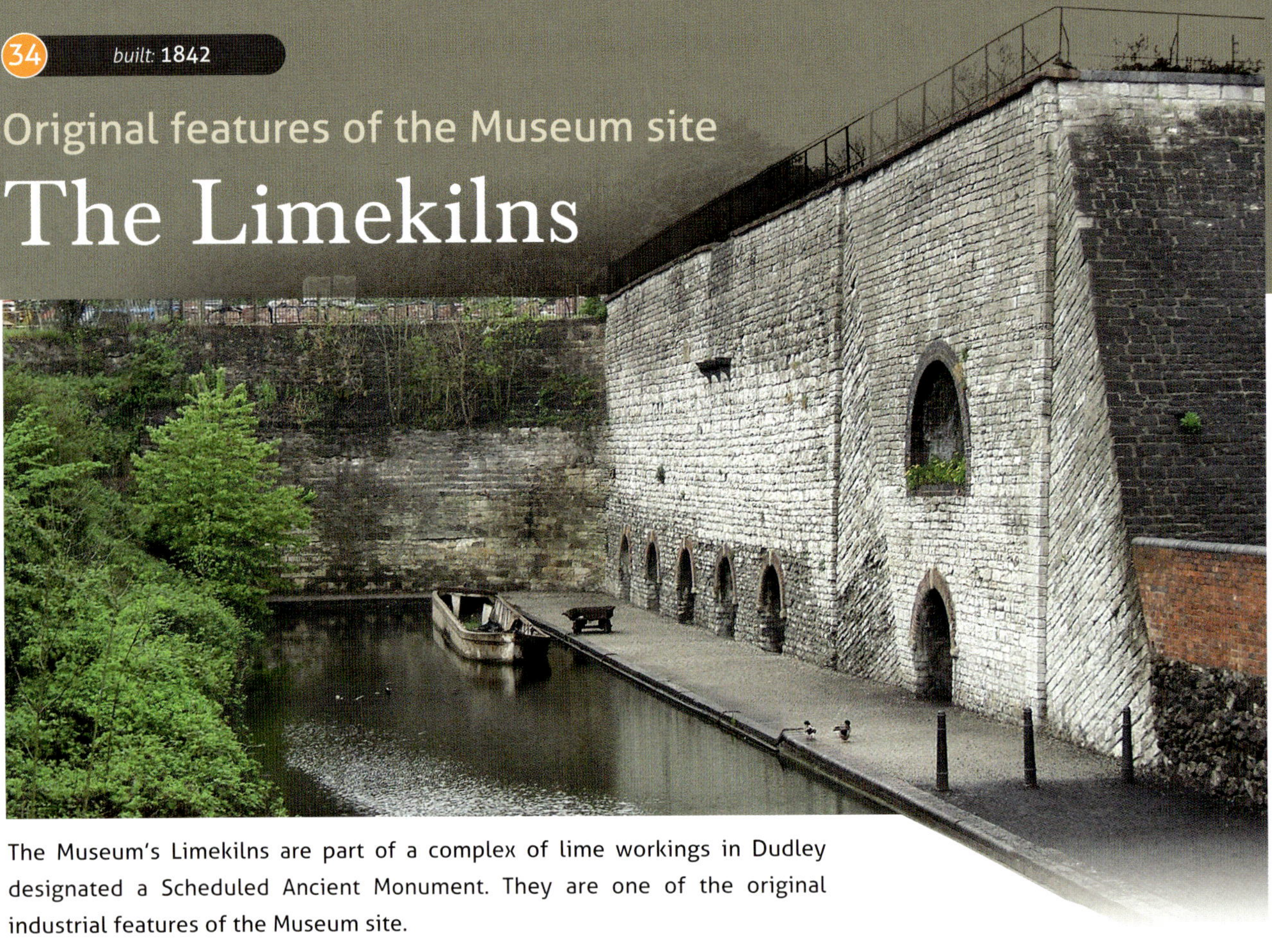

The Museum's Limekilns are part of a complex of lime workings in Dudley designated a Scheduled Ancient Monument. They are one of the original industrial features of the Museum site.

Limestone (calcium carbonate) is a sedimentary rock and when it is burned (or calcined) at very high temperatures, carbon dioxide is released and quicklime (calcium oxide) produced. When quicklime is mixed – or slaked – with water, a stable powder, slaked lime (calcium hydroxide) is obtained. Limestone, quicklime and slaked lime are often all referred to as 'lime' and there can be confusion between the three materials but each is a distinct chemical compound with different properties and applications. From at least Roman times lime has been used to make mortar but in the eighteenth century it was discovered that limestone could be used as a flux – that is, for drawing off the impurities as slag - in the production of iron in blast furnaces. This was to be vitally important for the expansion of iron production in the Black Country: as numbers of blast furnaces increased, so did the demand for limestone.

Limestone of the Silurian period – the 'Much Wenlock Beds' (actually consisting of two separate beds, the Thick and the Thin Beds) outcrops on two hills north of Dudley town centre, the Wren's Nest and Castle Hill. The limestone has been worked extensively for centuries and on the Museum site, a small area of the 'Thick Bed' limestone was worked under the extreme southern end (near the Museum entrance) in the early 1840s and the 'Thin Bed' worked under most of the site from 1846 to 1905.

The Limekilns were built in 1842 immediately south of earlier 'horseshoe kilns' located near the entrance to the Dudley Canal Tunnel 52. They consist of a bank of four massive continuous feed draw kilns accessed by their own canal arm and basin. Draw kilns were introduced in the mid-eighteenth century and enabled the coal and limestone to be fed continuously. There were originally three kilns with vertical brick shafts; a fourth and larger kiln was added c. 1865 to the east side of the bank; each kiln was surmounted by a large tapering brick chimney.

The limestone and coal was packed in alternate layers inside the kilns and a fire lit at the base. As the material burned, more coal and limestone was tipped in at the top and the quicklime extracted by labourers working in chambers at the bottom, reached through the arched openings off the tow path. It was dangerous work as the quicklime could cause serious burns and blindness. The coal and limestone were originally raised from the towpath by a horse powered winding engine or gin. A steam powered crane replaced the gin in the 1870s and this was also used to load the kilns from the top of the chimneys, the height of which was specially lowered for the purpose. By the 1920s most local sources of limestone were exhausted and the kilns ceased operation.

***Above:** The Limekilns and the Canal Arm*

***Right:** Detail of a watercolour sketch by Richard M Rayner (1843-1908) of the top of the Limekilns in 1865 showing the original brick chimneys and the horse gin*

The Canal Arm and Basin

The Canal Arm and Basin connecting the Limekilns with the Dudley Canal was built in 1839. It originally extended for half a mile eastwards before joining the Old Main Line from Wolverhampton to Birmingham. The original arm is now cut off where it runs under Birmingham New Road and the remains of a timber wharf boat, 'Billy' lies across the old junction and forms part of the path around the water's edge. Instead the canal now swings round to join the Dudley Canal passing the Boat Dock 68 which was apparently formed out of mining subsidence in the middle of the nineteenth century.

The arm now forms the southern boundary of the Village and is spanned by the Broad Street iron canal bridge from Wolverhampton 37 . Several of the Museum's boats are usually moored in the Canal Arm and these are mostly the unglamorous day boats which typified the canal traffic of the region.

The Canal Arm looking towards the Canal Street Bridge with the Limekilns beyond and the Rolling Mill on the right

36 *first installed:* **1865**

Entrance to the Museum village

The Penfold Letter Box

Letter boxes arrived on our streets in the 1850s and the contract for making the first national standard design in 1859 was awarded to Cochrane & Co of Dudley.

Cochrane, Grove & Company also made the Penfold type of pillar box which was designed by the architect, J W Penfold (1828-1909) and introduced in 1866. Over a hundred of these distinctive hexagonal boxes survive. There were five different types and three sizes and the Museum's example is the largest size of the commonest fourth type which has the aperture placed below the Royal coat of arms and a moulded surround to the collection plate. This particular box was installed on the corner of Baker Street and Blandford Street, London in 1865.

Alexander Cochrane built the Woodside Iron Works and Foundry in 1841. It soon established itself as one of the largest works on the Earl of Dudley's Estates: they made the huge cast-iron columns for the Crystal Palace in 1850 and also parts for several bridges including Brunel's Clifton Suspension Bridge in Bristol. This letter box of about 1870 along with the post of the gas lamp in front of the Station Road Cottages, dated 1866, are two of their smaller products which, nevertheless, serve as a reminder of this once famous ironworks which finally closed in 1939.

37 *erected* **1879**

Canal Street Bridge *originally from* Broad Street, Wolverhampton

This bridge of cast and wrought-iron was erected in 1879 to carry what was then Canal Street (later Broad Street) over the Birmingham Canal in Wolverhampton. It was designed by Eastlake Thoms, the Borough Engineer, to replace an existing masonry bridge and built by Tildesley of Willenhall. The bridge was dismantled in 1976 and was one of the first structures to be rebuilt on the Museum site.

The Canal Street Bridge at its original location photographed c. 1950 as a Wolverhampton Corporation trolley bus crosses

Above: *The massive cast-iron arches of the Canal Street Bridge seen from the towpath under the bridge*

Inset: *Wolverhampton Corporation plaque, 1879*

Lawrence Lane, Old Hill

Gregory's General Store

Gregory's General Store occupies the two front rooms of a pair of houses, numbers 89 and 90 Lawrence Lane, Old Hill. Originally they were separated by a central tunnel to the back yard.

The houses were built by Charles Gregory, who worked for H & T Danks, iron boat and boiler makers in Netherton. Originally let out to tenants, the Gregory family soon moved into one of the houses themselves and Charles' wife, Mary, set up a grocery business. In the early 1900s, the entire building was converted to a double fronted shop with living accommodation upstairs for the family.

Mrs Gregory held a wide selection of stock and catered for those on low earnings struggling to make ends meet. It was common for essential weekly items such as eggs to be sold individually and for tea, butter and paraffin by the penny's worth. Meat and dairy produce was sold from the counter on the right of the shop and included bacon, ham, butter, cheese, margarine, beef suet, pork fat, lard, scratchings, homemade faggots and mushy peas, tripe and cowheels. The family kept their own pigs and chickens which were reared for the shop. Groceries and greengrocery was sold from the centre counter – the majority of vegetables were displayed outside the front of the shop in baskets on the pavement. The left counter was used for the sale of a wide range of goods including sweets, drapery and cigarettes.

The shop remained in the Gregory family until 1936 when it became Parkin's Shop. It finally closed around 1976. Scheduled for demolition, it was dismantled brick by brick and moved to the Museum in 1979-80. The shop interior is set in 1913 and lit by gas. The fitting out was guided by Charles and Mary's granddaughter, Gwen Jenkins, who vividly remembered the layout of the store from her childhood; her parents moved into the shop in 1917. The former store room at the back has been reconstructed as the family parlour and a double brewhouse based on the original one constructed in the back yard.

39 setting: 1913

Gregory's Brew House

In the back yard the double Brew House, based on the original was used by the family for running water, laundry and to store shop stock. The family baked their own bread in the ovens to sell in the shop and used the boiler to make tripe. The tripe, made from a pig's stomach cleaned and scalded and combined with milk and onions, was kept warm in the Brew House and brought into the shop in a pot a bit at a time to be sold.

Top: *Gregory's General Store with vegetables displayed on the street; the tunnel or 'gunnel' on the left leads to the back yard and brewhouse.*

Centre: *A detail of the meat and dairy counter*

Bottom Right: *The Brew House can be found behind Gregory's General Store via the alley way to the left.*

40 setting: c.1910

Lawrence Lane, Old Hill

Anchor Maker's House

This house is one of a pair, built c. 1885 that used to stand at 91 and 92 Lawrence Lane, Old Hill.

The houses were condemned by the local council in the mid-1970s and dismantled by the Museum in 1978. Just one of the pair – Number 91 – was rebuilt at the Museum along with the side entry providing direct access to the back yard. It has the distinction of being the first house to be rebuilt on the Museum site. As the houses had been modernised, original fittings, including firegrates and fireplace surrounds were taken from 101 and 102, an identical pair of houses a few doors away.

Number 91 is an example of the 'byelaw house' – a type of working class town housing – usually built in terraces – built from the 1870s which was subject to legislation at national and local level aimed chiefly at improving standards of public health. Better standards of construction and sanitation and the provision of adequate space, front and back were enforced through local by-laws and distinguish these houses, therefore, from the earlier types of urban housing represented by the **Station Road Cottages** 55 and the **Brook Street Back-to-backs** 58.

It is a two up two down 'through' house with a back door opening onto a back yard. The front room was reserved for best whilst everyday living took place around the range in the kitchen. Stairs from the kitchen led to the two bedrooms. Similar houses were built all over urban England and Wales although a separate wash house – or brewhouse – was a particular feature of working class housing in the Black Country.

The houses were built by Charles Harper, an iron puddler, and let out to tenants. From 1902 Number 91 was occupied by Edward Parkin, who was described as a fitter in 1906 and an anchor worker in 1914. In 1912 the house was described as 'better class' with a wash house, earth closet and a 'good garden'. Occupants of neighbouring houses at this period included a collier, an ironworker, boiler maker, ships tackle maker, anchor smith, swivel maker, several chain makers, a road worker, bricklayer and various foundry workers. The house has been reconstructed as it might have been in c. 1910 by which time it is likely the house had gas and mains water.

41 setting: c.1910

Back Yard Chain Shop *from* Claremont Road, Old Hill

The Chain Shop was taken from the rear of 22 Claremont Street in Old Hill and was originally used to make oddwork 17 but is reconstructed to represent a typical small back yard chain shop for the making of small chain. It was built in the 1890s and originally had two identical hearths one of which was subsequently moved and replaced with a work bench.

Chain making was concentrated in the area around Cradley Heath. Whilst heavy and medium chains were made by men in large chainworks, lighter chains generally made from iron rods of less than 3/8 inch in diameter, were mostly made by outworkers in small shops attached to homes. The iron rods were supplied by the proprietors of the large chainworks or dealers and then worked up into chain in the back yard or 'brewhouse' chain shops which were found behind many houses in Cradley Heath.

In 1910, there were about 3,500 small chainmakers of which about two thirds were women. They made everything from watch chain to 'country work' – chain used by farmers – including the traces of horse drawn ploughs. They were very poorly paid on piece rates according to the amount and weight of chain they produced. They worked long hours – sometimes more than fourteen hours a day and were paid a pittance. Wages improved markedly after the ten week strike of 1910 33 but it remained hot and dirty work which for many women had to be combined with domestic chores and looking after babies and young children.

After the First World War, the development of electrically welded machine-made small chain caused the rapid decline of the domestic trade although a few back yard chain shops were still at work in the 1950s. The last female chain maker was Mrs Lucy Woodhall who worked for Samuel Woodhouse & Sons of Cradley Heath; she retired in 1973 at the age of 73 after working for more than 60 years in the trade.

Top:* *91 Lawrence Lane at the Museum; *the tunnel entrance on the right leads to the back yard Chain Shop*

Top left: *The kitchen of the* **Anchor Maker's House**

Top right: *Clockwork bottle jack for rotating meat roasting in front of an open fire; made by George Salter & Co., West Bromwich*

Centre left: *The Front Parlour*

Above: *Wallet of sample chains from Samuel Lewis & Co., Netherton*

Above: *Babies and young children were often part of the scene when women were at work making chain*

Halesowen Road, Netherton

Emile Doo's Chemist Shop

The building housing Doo's Chemist's Shop is a replica of the shop owned by Harold Emile Doo at 358 Halesowen Road, Netherton.

The original building was built in 1886 and was originally a tailor's shop. James Emile Doo began business in Netherton in 1882 and his son, Harold Emile Doo, took over having qualified as a pharmacist in c. 1918. In 1929 he moved the premises across the road to Number 358 and from there he carried out his business until ill health forced his retirement in May 1968. The shop lay untouched until his death two years later and then in 1973 the fittings and stock were donated to the Museum. When the replica shop was being built using bricks reclaimed from two properties in Pearson Street, Old Hill, the Museum was able to acquire the original shop front from Doo's premises.

Before the formation of the National Health Service in 1948, local chemists' shops like Doo's played a central role in the local community, offering free medical advice; babies and diabetics were weighed weekly at the shop, and administering basic first aid. Emile Doo made his own remedies such as 'Doo's Infant Preservative' and also undertook veterinary work and dentistry in the back room.

With guidance from Emile Doo's daughter, Betty, the shop has been laid out as it was shortly after the move across the road in 1929. The shop is lit by gas and the shelves are filled with the original jars and bottles including the large round glass carboys (see above) used to hold liquids. Pill making equipment is demonstrated at the counter.

Emille Doo's shop photographed at its original location in Halesowen Road, Netherton

The interior contains the original fitted shelves and cabinets like this one behind the counter which contains 52 drawers, each with glass handles and labelled with the Latin names of the medicines they contained

44 built: 1837

Darby Hand, near Netherton

Providence Chapel

The Darby Hand New Connexion Methodist Chapel was originally opened on 29 January 1837.

Methodism had emerged in the mid-eighteenth century through the preaching of John Wesley (1703-91) who made 15 visits to Dudley and other parts of the Black Country from 1749. Methodism challenged the conventional teachings of the Church of England and held a particular appeal for the poor; and its great expansion after 1790 was in the mining and manufacturing districts of Britain. The timing was crucial. At the very moment that the pace of industrial development on the South Staffordshire coalfield accelerated, Methodism and other nonconformist sects, such as the Baptists and the Unitarians, took hold to become a deeply rooted part of working class culture whilst their chapels became a recognisable part of the Black Country townscape.

The small settlement of Darby End grew in the late eighteenth century as a coal mining community alongside the Dudley Canal. It was named after a family who arrived in the area in the sixteenth century to run a mill on the Mousesweet Brook. In the nineteenth century this area was also commonly referred to as Darby Hand and it is by this name that the chapel is generally known. Darby Hand Chapel was built as a place of worship for the Methodist New Connexion which had split from the Wesleyan Methodists in 1797. Like many nonconformist chapels, the building consists of a simple rectangle built of brick and has two small rear extensions. The front is relieved by an imposing entrance of rendered brick. The interior is relatively plain and functional with a small lobby underneath a gallery that runs down the sides and the rear of the chapel. The side galleries are supported by fluted columns with ornate capitals that divide the interior into a nave flanked by aisles. The dominant feature of the interior is, of course, the tall pulpit which ensured the minister could be seen by his entire congregation. It stands below a scrolled banner painted on the wall which proclaims, 'Worship the Lord In the Beauty of Holiness'.

The chapel closed down in 1974 and was one of the first structures to be rebuilt at the Museum between 1977 and 1979. Services in the Chapel are arranged by The Friends of the Museum throughout the year and include a Sunday School Anniversary and Harvest Festival.

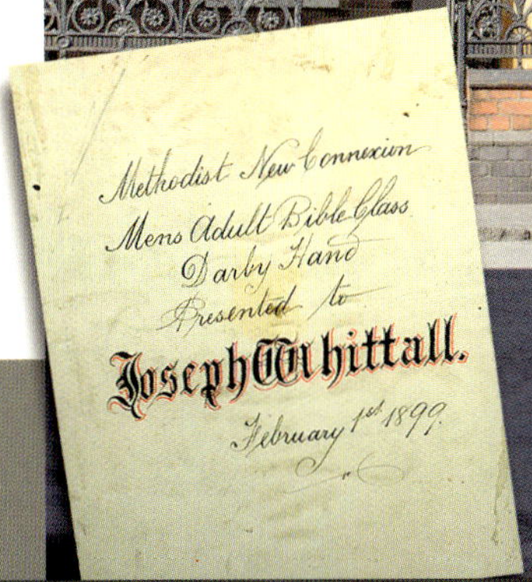

Book plate from a bible presented by the Methodists at Darby Hand to Joseph Wittall in 1899

Top: *The chapel pulpit*
Centre: *The pulpit framed by the side galleries*

T. Cook's Sweet Shop

The Sweet Shop occupies one half of a replica of 48 and 50 Birmingham Street, Oldbury, two shops built in c. 1845. Number 48 has been reconstructed as a traditional sweet shop with a rear work room and named after the shop run by Thomas Cook and his family at 21 Bond Street, Dudley from 1871 -1901. The period setting is c. 1900.

The making of sweets was a simple and inexpensive business. A mixture of sugar and glucose was boiled in large copper pans on a confectioner's furnace similar to a domestic wash boiler. For making drops and rock the sugar needed to reach a temperature of 157 degrees centigrade. Care was needed to avoid burning the sugar. When the sugar was molten it was poured onto a well oiled pouring plate of cast-iron which was warmed so that the molten sugar – referred to as 'toffee' – was kept soft and workable. The toffee was kneaded on the plate - colours and flavours added – and then passed through the 'drop machine'. Resembling a small mangle, this was equipped with interchangeable brass rollers that rolled out the toffee strips into different shapes ranging from simple ovals to bees and fish. When the rolled strips of toffee had cooled they were broken up and smoothed off by being tossed in a riddle. The equipment in the sweetshop belonged to George Hutchings who used it in Stirchley, Birmingham from 1943-88 making his own brands of sweets but also the old favourites such as pear drops and acid drops.

Top: The heavy brass rollers which fit into the drop machine to press out the final shape of the sweets

***Veal's Baker's Shop**, left and **Thomas Cook's Sweet Shop**, right*

Glass sweet jars containing traditional boiled sweets

46 *setting:* **c.1900**

Birmingham Street, Oldbury

Veal's Baker's Shop

Next to the Sweet Shop is Veal's Bakery Shop which was carried on at this address, 50 Birmingham Street, Oldbury from the 1870s. George Veal, a confectioner, bought the shop in 1879 and after his death in 1884, his wife married Arthur Smith and the properties remained in the family until the 1920s.

The shop window lettering for Veal, Cadbury's and Fry's chocolate, together with the royal arms denoting the royal warrants these two makers held, is a replica of the original lettering which was made of enamelled copper and puttied to the window glass. The shop sold the bread baked at the **bakery** at the rear of the shop 61. The shop supplemented its sales of bread with biscuits, whole and broken and it would seem likely that chocolate was also sold in the shop in Veal's time. The shop also sold Johnston's British Wine (a fortified wine) at 2/6 ($12\frac{1}{2}$p) a bottle and customers were able to have a glass of wine and a biscuit on the premises for threepence (1p).

The shop is set in c. 1900 and behind the shop is a gas lit parlour with a kitchen range and a back kitchen.

Top: *Veal's Baker's Shop in c. 1910*

Above: *Traditional cakes and biscuits are sold in the Baker's Shop*

47 *setting:* c.1910

Pawnbroker's Shop

The building in which the Pawnbroker's Shop has been reconstructed is one of a pair of cottages from School Lane in Himley on the very western edge of the Black Country.

The cottages were built in the 1840s and one was known to have operated for some years as a corner shop. Many pawnbroking concerns operated from converted houses and so the setting of this display within these cottages is designed to represent a small scale business. The shop takes its name from a particularly well known Black Country pawnbroking family business – that of Joseph Wiltshire – founded in Great Bridge in the early 1900s.

Pawning goods to quickly raise a short term loan was established by the eleventh century as the most ready source of credit for the poor. The articles pawned were taken as security for a loan, the value of which was based on what the pawnbroker thought he could raise by selling the goods outright. The customer received the loan and a ticket and to redeem the pledge had to pay the loan in full plus various charges including the cost of the ticket and the valuation. Following the 1872 Pawnbroker's Act, the charges for services and the rates of interest were fixed. All pledges were kept by law for a year. After this time the pledge became forfeit and the pawnbroker was allowed to sell the goods to make good the loan he had paid out. For those constantly struggling to make ends meet the pawnshop provided a means of obtaining a simple bridging loan for a few days: thus some families would pawn linen most weeks on Monday and redeem it the following Friday or Saturday. Pawnbrokers were usually located in large urban working class districts where wages were low and not always stable. Not surprisingly, therefore, they were once numerous in the Black Country: in 1870 there were 160 in the region. Some businesses combined pawnbroking with retailing. In this reconstruction unredeemed goods and other stock are sold in the front room whilst the pawning of goods was done in greater privacy in the 'pledge room' at the back.

In the back yard of the two houses a brewhouse from Birch Coppice, Quarry Bank has been reconstructed along with privies and ash pits which have been built using materials from the originals which stood behind the houses in Himley.

48 *setting:* c.1920

The Village Fried Fish Shop

49 *setting:* c.1915

The Greengrocer's Shop

The building is a replica of two shops out of a row of three in Lower Lichfield Street, Willenhall before 1848. The Museum building represents Numbers 39 and 40.

The Willenhall shops were originally built as houses and converted into front room shops in the early 1900s. From about 1916 until the early 1930s, Number 39 was a greengrocer's shop belonging to Gertrude Adey, wife of a Willenhall locksmith, and Number 40 was a fried fish shop.

The frying range and fittings in Number 40 come from a fish and chip shop at 49 Old Birchills in Walsall which operated from 1933 to 1954. The range was originally coal fired and made by Walker & Husler, sheet metal workers of Birmingham between 1926 and 1930.

Left: *The three golden balls – the long established trade sign of pawn brokers - is associated with the arms of the Italian Medici family, the ruling Florentine family who started as bankers and money lenders*

Below: *Gertrude Adey (born 1876)*

50 *setting:* **c.1930**

The Hardware & Ironmonger's Shop

The Ironmonger's Shop and Hardware Shop occupy two properties which formerly stood on the corner of Piper's Row and Tower Street in Wolverhampton.

They were built c. 1829 and Number 1 Tower Street – now the Ironmonger's Shop – served originally as a grocery and tea dealer whilst Number 34 Piper's Row, the Hardware Store, was occupied by a coachbuilder. To accommodate the building on the Museum site the two sides of the building were reversed, thus placing Piper's Row where Tower Street was and vice versa. Nevertheless, the brickwork on the Piper's Row elevation was carefully reconstructed preserving the original painted advertisement for Gold Flake tobacco.

The shop front was copied from a former wet fish shop in Owen Street, Tipton and the shop contents have been collected to represent a typical hardware shop of c. 1930. The stock includes a selection of household equipment – tin baths, pots and pans, tableware, lamps, laundry irons and hearth equipment – most of which was made in the West Midlands.

The corner Ironmonger's Shop is a reconstruction of a typical Black Country ironmonger's shop created by using original fittings from Nash's ironmonger's shop in Oldbury which occupied a corner location in Church Street. The business had been established by Thomas Nash in 1860 and was subsequently taken over by his son, Isaac and when he died in 1951, the business was carried on by his business partner, Frank Bridge. When the shop finally closed in 1984 the interior looked very much as it might have done c. 1900 with jumbled shelves, window and counter display cabinets and an old wooden counter. These items were adapted for the new interior and the shop filled with appropriate stock obtained from local manufactures and retailers. The result is an atmospheric recreation of a small ironmonger's shop of c. 1930 packed with builder's equipment, edge tools, screws, nails and other items which were sold loose.

Top: *The **Hardware Shop** on the corner of Piper's Row (left) and Tower Street (right)*

Above: *Rebuilt at the Museum showing the advertisement for W.D. & H.O. Wills Gold Flake preserved on the wall*

The shop contents typify the range of goods stocked by hardware shops in the 1920s and 1930s

51 *setting:* **c.1937**

Sidebotham's Steel Trap Works, Wednesfield

The Steel Trap works, owned by four generations of the Sidebotham family, is a unique survival of a metal working trade particularly associated with Wednesfield. By 1865, when there were about fifteen animal trap makers in the town, William Sidebotham (born c. 1840) had established premises on Rookery Street. The business expanded and in 1913 a new larger workshop was built which brought together the various stages of production under one roof. Traps of all sizes from large bear traps – an example can be seen on the workshop floor – to small rabbit traps were made and most were exported: the overseas destinations can be seen marked on the stencils.

Trap making had traditionally involved skilled forge work but Sidebotham's adoption of hand and power presses in the 1930s enabled the introduction of semi-skilled factory production. Three power presses driven by flat belts and overhead line shafting are located near the entrance. They were used for most of the cutting, piercing and bending of the larger trap parts such as the stock and jaws and were powered by a gas engine; the existing single cylinder gas engine of 1905 was made by Tangye of Smethwick. Further down the central section are the hand operated fly presses which were used to carry out small bending, curling and riveting jobs. The power presses were considered light enough to be operated by women and Sidebotham always employed a large female labour force. Forges, however, were always used to make the trap springs. Once assembled the traps were taken in wheelbarrows to the warehouse for packing and covered in a protective mixture of paraffin and mineral oil.

The Trap Shop is remembered as a friendly place to work with men and women working alongside members of the Sidebotham family. It was also a noisy and hot environment with the heat of the forges, the din of the overhead shafting, the crunching of the power presses and the clatter of the trap parts dropping into work pans. Following closure, the Museum was offered the building and much of the machinery in 1982. The original structure, with its latticework Belfast type roof trusses, had to be considerably shortened to fit its new location at the Museum. The reconstruction is set in the late 1930s.

Top: *The interior of the Trap Shop*

Right: *Two large animal traps from the Trap Shop and a stencil for Nairobi*

52 *from:* **1769-1951**

Canal Tunnel and the Birmingham Canal Navigations

The Museum's Canal Arm is spanned by Brown's Bridge at its junction with the main canal network.

This particular stretch of canal was built as part of the Dudley Canal and is known as the Dudley Number 1 Canal. To the left the canal disappears into the confined space of the Dudley Tunnel at the Tipton Portal whilst to the right after a short distance it joins the Old Main Line - part of the oldest canal in the Black Country - which runs between Wolverhampton and Birmingham. It was promoted by the Birmingham Canal Company and engineered by James Brindley. It was opened in stages between 1769 and 1772 and extends for over 22 miles from Aldersley, north of Wolverhampton, on the Staffordshire & Worcester Canal to the centre of Birmingham.

The Tipton end of the main Tunnel alongside the Museum was originally built as a mine tunnel between 1776-78 to enable the limestone to be brought out by boat. It was known as Lord Ward's Tunnel and originally terminated underground at the Castle Mill Basin. From here other subterranean canals were subsequently built to connect with other underground workings each distinguished with its own name, such as 'Dark Cavern' and 'Singing Cavern'.

Work soon began on extending Lord Ward's tunnel under Dudley to Park Head. Here the canal descended a flight of five locks to join the terminal basin of the Dudley Canal at Blowers Green. After seven years work the through tunnel, 3,154 yards long, was opened in 1792. Like many early canal tunnels there was no towpath so boats had to be 'legged' through the tunnel by the boatmen lying on their backs and pushing with their feet against the walls; the horse, meanwhile, was walked over the top of the hill.

In 1846 the Dudley Company joined the Birmingham Canal Navigations (the BCN). The canal was heavily used and in 1853, 41,000 boats passed through the tunnel but after 1858, following the opening of the much larger Netherton Tunnel, which ran parallel, traffic declined. By the mid nineteenth century the limestone in the underground workings was beginning to run out and some of the abandoned caverns were used as tourist features. Lord Dudley installed gas lighting in Dark Cavern and used it for concerts, balls and lectures. Traffic ceased altogether in 1951 after which the canal became derelict. It was restored in 1973 by Dudley Canal Trust. Today boat trips organised by Dudley Canal Trust (Trips) Ltd take visitors through the Castle Mill Basin which has now lost its original roof and through to Singing Cavern.

***Top:** The Dudley Canal looking towards Tipton Junction where it joins the Old Main Line running from Wolverhampton to Birmingham*

The maximum depth of the Dudley Tunnel below ground is 180 feet

The Tipton Portal of the Dudley Canal

Centre left: *Legging in the Dudley Tunnel, c. 1890*

Centre right: *A replica of a trolley used in the underground quarries to transport blocks of limestone*

Above: *The Tunnel is 13 feet high with typically five feet of water and eight feet of head room*

Horses and the Black Country

Carter's Yard

The Carter's Yard serves as a reminder of the contribution of horse transport to the economic development of the Black Country. In the nineteenth century horses were used to pull coal wagons and carts, narrow boats, trams, goods to and from railway stations, private carriages and cabs and – out of sight for most – in the coal mines, ponies drew tubs laden with coal to the pit bottom. From the 1920s the use of horses declined as electric trams, motorised canal boats, motor lorries, vans, cars and motorcycles relegated horse drawn traffic to a minor role.

The Carter's Yard is immediately to the left of the Bottle & Glass Inn. The first building on the left is the Harness Room, a single storey brick building containing a cast-iron stove and tack. The combined office and tack room is based on two buildings in Netherton, now much altered, which are believed to have been used by contractors who often did business as hauliers and undertakers. Next to the Harness Room is a stable with two stalls and an overhead hay loft which stood in the back yard of a cottage on Ogley Hay Road, Burntwood, Cannock and was probably built about 1900. The stable fittings were donated from a coach house and stables in Handsworth Wood Road, Birmingham. Beyond the stable is a large covered area with one open side which was a cart shed but is now used to stable one of the horses. The last building in the range is a loose box with a hayrack and manger.

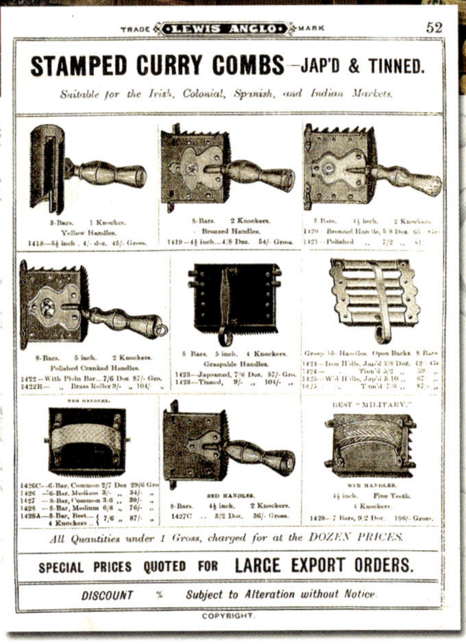

TRADE LEWIS ANGLO MARK 52

STAMPED CURRY COMBS—JAP'D & TINNED.

Suitable for the Irish, Colonial, Spanish, and Indian Markets.

3-Bars. 1 Knocker. Yellow Handles.
1418—5½ inch . 4/- doz. 45/- Gross.

8-Bars. 2 Knockers. Bronzed Handles.
1419—4½ inch...4/8 Doz. 54/- Gross.

8-Bars. 5 inch. 2 Knockers. Polished Cranked Handles.
1422—With Plain Bar...7/6 Doz 87/- Gro.
1422R— „ Brass Roller 9/- „ 104/- „

8 Bars. 5 inch. 4 Knockers. Graspable Handles.
1423—Japanned, 7/6 Doz. 87/- Gro.
1423—Tinned, 9/- „ 104/- „

WEB HANDLES.
1426C—6-Bar, Common 2/7 Doz 29/6 Gro
1426 —6-Bar, Medium 3/- „ 34/- „
1427 —8-Bar, Common 3/6 „ 39/- „
1428 —8-Bar, Medium 6/8 „ 76/- „
1428A—8-Bar, Best... 4 Knockers.. 7/6 „ 87/- „

RED HANDLES.
8-Bars 4½ inch. 2 Knockers.
1427C .. 3/2 Doz. 36/- Gross.

BEST "MILITARY."
WEB HANDLES.
4½ inch. Fine Teeth. 4 Knockers.
1429—7 Bars, 9/2 Doz. 106/- Gross.

All Quantities under 1 Gross, charged for at the DOZEN PRICES.

SPECIAL PRICES QUOTED FOR LARGE EXPORT ORDERS.

DISCOUNT % Subject to Alteration without Notice

COPYRIGHT.

Top: *The Harness Room*

Above: *A typical coal merchants cart c.1900*

Buckpool, Brierley Hill

Bottle and Glass Inn

The Bottle and Glass Inn stood originally by the junction of Moor Street and Leys Road on Brierley Hill Road, Buckpool and backed on to the Stourbridge Canal at the top of the Sixteen Locks. The exact date of construction is not known but it was probably built shortly after the canal was cut between 1776 and 1779.

The symmetrical layout of the front entrance is probably original; the door case with its simple pediment may also be original and even, perhaps, the two ground bays windows but the overriding sense is of a Regency facade. The creamy white stucco wall extending upwards to a flat parapet wall hiding the pitched roof and the scrolled brackets – or consoles – above the first floor windows are clearly of the period 1820-40. It is possible that alterations to the building coincided with changes of ownership. In the early 1820s the building appears on a map as 'The Bush' but by the 1840s it was 'The Bottle and Glass', the name it retained until closure in 1979.

Inside and to the left of the front door is the main bar with a plain wooden counter, scrubbed floor sprinkled with sawdust and cast-iron stove. It is lit by paraffin lamps and candles. To the right is the snug. This has a quarry tiled floor, a large open fire place with a high mantle shelf and an original elm settle opposite the window; the back room is a later addition.

Instances of drunkenness and disreputable behaviour punctuate the history of the pub. In 1857, Henry Wiggin, the landlord was fined five shillings for selling alcohol 'during the hours of divine service' and in 1871, William Mullet, a boatman and landlord of the pub was charged with permitting drunkenness in his house. When another case of drunkenness went to court in 1912, the police described the pub as 'thoroughly uninhabitable'. Mr and Mrs Hilton ran the pub between 1914 and 1928 when it was a tied house owned by the Hereford and Tredegar Brewery: it was frequented by miners, glass cutters and by boatmen who often stayed there throughout the day, leaving their horses to graze in the garden at the back. The pub was then open for all day drinking and it was not uncommon for fights to erupt. It is recalled that the pub was not considered a suitable place for women at this time!

The Hereford and Tredegar Brewery was taken over by Ansells in 1937 and it was they who presented the building to the Museum following closure in 1979. The Bottle and Glass Inn continues to function as a pub, its interior set in 1915 serving traditional cask conditioned beers from several local breweries.

Top: *At its original location the* ***Bottle & Glass*** *originally contained a yard on the right as in the reconstruction*

Above: *The Snug*

55 *setting:* **c.1900**

Station Road, Old Hill

Station Road Cottages

These two cottages are replicas of houses which still stand – albeit much modified – on Station Road in Old Hill and near the former Great Western Railway station for Old Hill. They were built in 1848 and formed part of the Earl of Dudley's estates. They were typical industrial dwellings of the time with three rooms including a ground floor kitchen and pantry and a single first floor bedroom. The two cottages originally shared a central chimney stack but they were extended at different times to provide more accommodation.

The original occupants were Joseph Rose, a colliery banksman (a man who lands the skip of coal at the surface) and Timothy Newton, a nail maker. Remarkably, direct descendants of the Newton family lived in the houses until 1966 and recollections provided by surviving members of the family enabled the Museum to accurately reconstruct the interiors of the two houses as they were in the early 1900s.

Wiliam Rose occupied the left hand cottage, Number 97 (renumbered 138 in 1948) and lived there until 1877 and after a succession of different occupiers, Samuel Newton moved in with his wife, Florence, in 1903. Samuel was a horse driver and had eleven children. The family kept pigs around the back in a sty: the one rebuilt at the Museum is not the original but one taken from a house at Chapel Street, Lye and dates to about 1890. The boiler on the side was used for boiling pig swill. The pig was salted by the family and the sides of ham, covered in muslin, were hung up on the stairs. The brewhouse on the side of the house was not only used for washing but for brewing beer and baking which Florence did fortnightly. The kitchen contained a table, sofa and wooden bench under the window; there was a clock, Singer sewing machine and an oil lamp which hung from the ceiling. It is recalled that there were always two kettles on the boil hanging over the kitchen range fire. Unusually, the parlour was in frequent use and contained an organ: this particular one comes from a house in Wednesfield.

Next door at Number 98 (subsequently renumbered 136) the original occupant, Timothy Newton, lived there with his wife Elizabeth and when he died in 1851, his widow, Elizabeth, married Romantiezer Plant, another nail maker. He lived there until 1885 and then Thomas Newton, the son of Timothy and Elizabeth took over the cottage with his wife, Emma. In later years, Emma – by then known as 'Granny Newton' – ran a small shop from the house and this has been reconstructed as a shoe repair shop and filled with tools and equipment from Lawrence Davies's business at 24 Bristol Street, Wolverhampton.

Right: *The kitchen of the left hand cottage, Number 97*

Top Right: *Emma ('Granny') Newton who lived at 96 Station Road and the houses c. 1900*

56 *setting:* c.1910

Station Road, Old Hill

The Coal Yard

This reconstruction of a Coal Yard is based on evidence collected from several Black Country coal merchants and dealers. Small yards selling coal could be found in almost every neighbourhood catering for domestic consumers and small businesses such as bakeries, sweet shops and fish friers. Most people used coal for cooking, laundering and room heating and could consume as much as two hundred weight (over 100 kg) a week.

Coal dealers tended to be smaller scale than coal merchants and often combined the business with another trade such as haulage. The coal dealers normally held a stock of a few tons collected directly from the land-sale wharf at the local colliery using a two wheeled horse drawn tipper cart which could carry a $^3/_4$ ton load. The coalmen's horses were generally fell ponies or 'half legged', a cross between a cob and a shire.

Most dealers operated delivery rounds using a four wheeled flat bed wagon. Coal was delivered loose or in hundred weight bags of hemp or jute, waterproofed with Stockholm tar. Loose coal was tipped directly on the pavement for the householder to move or to shovel down a coal hole to a cellar. Coal merchants would also cater for casual sales or 'barrow' sales and these small quantities – sometimes just a quarter of half a hundred weight – were collected by the customer in wheel barrows, improvised trolleys or prams. Some purchases were just enough to make an evening's fire. Larger merchants stocked all grades of coal from slack to nuts to the larger cobbles and lumps. Many customers preferred 'good lump coal' which burned slowly and could be used to keep the fire in the grate overnight.

By the late 1920s the scene was changing: horses began to give way to motor lorries and as the smaller local collieries gradually closed dealers turned to the larger merchants for their supplies. They were usually based in a railway station yard or canal basin and obtained their coal from the three large collieries of Baggeridge, Sandwell Park and Hamstead on the Staffordshire Thick 9 or from further afield.

***Above:** Advertisement from Blockridge's Dudley Almanac, 1928*

***Top:** The Coal Yard with a typical coal merchant's cart*

***Top inset:** Pushing coal home in prams c. 1950*

57 setting: c.1926

Harts Hill, Brierley Hill

Limelight Cinema

The Limelight Cinema is an example of a small family run cinema typical of the period 1910-20 although it did not open until 30 August 1921. It was owned by John Henry Revill, an engineer with Cartwright & Paddock and tucked away behind a row of houses on Vine Street in Harts Hill. Access was through wooden gates, down an alley past John Revill's home.

It consists of a plain brick structure and in compliance with the Cinematography Act of 1909 it originally had a separate wooden projection room because of the fire hazard from the highly inflammable cellulose nitrate film then in use. The auditorium was lit by gas and could seat up to 103 people on plain wooden benches. Mrs Revill sold the 'tuppence ha'penny' (1p) and 'fivepenny tickets' (2p) from a small wooden pay booth tacked onto the end of the building. A gas engine shed contained two gas engines, a Crossley Type K horizontal engine and a Tangye, made in Smethwick.

The cinema proved a success and in 1926 was extended. 18 tip-up seats were added and the two original second hand projectors – a Dreadnought Bioscope and a 1912 Ememann Bioscope – were replaced by two new Kamm projectors, a Motiograph and an Ememann, These were equipped with very bright and powerful carbon arc lamps and it is likely, therefore, that the gas engines were installed at this time to provide the necessary power.

The cinema showed silent films to a musical accompaniment of records played on a wind up gramophone by Violet, John Revill's eldest daughter. Films at The Limelight included Charlie Chaplin comedies, feature length Westerns and cliff hanging serials but from the start of 1929, the cinema struggled. By then, new luxury cinemas had opened in Dudley and Brierley Hill showing the new 'talkies'. John Revill could no longer compete and in July 1929 the cinema closed. The building was then used to breed

and sell tropical fish until John Revill died in 1965.

The interior of the cinema has been refitted as closely as possible to its appearance following the addition of the 1926 extension. The benches are replicas of the one original bench to survive but the tip seats are new, the originals having been removed after the cinema closed. The wooden porch is based on a drawing of the original and contains a display which includes one of the original Kamm carbon arc projectors.

***Above:** The basic interior of the auditorium*

***Centre right** The cinema at its original location in Brierley Hill*

58 *setting:* **1890 & 1924**

Brook Street, Woodsetton

The Back-to-Backs

***Fish tail** gas light, 10 Brook Street*

Houses built back to back under one roof so that each had no back door or back windows were built in large numbers through the nineteenth century in the industrial areas of the midlands and the north as a means of providing cheap, high density housing for the working classes. When this block was rescued from Brook Street in Woodsetton by the Museum in c. 1990, it was believed to be the last example of this house type surviving in the Black Country.

The houses were built about 1852 by John Jevon, a colliery 'charter master' 9. Number 12 on the right hand side of the entry was built as a through house with two ground floor rooms and front and back doors. Numbers 10 and 11 were built back-to-back and consist of just one ground floor kitchen with a small pantry and two bedrooms above. There were originally brewhouses and privies behind 11 and 12. Number 12 is set in 1924 whilst Numbers 10 and 11 are furnished to represent their condition in 1890, currently the earliest date for any interior at the Museum. In 1891 the tenant in Number 11 was Henry Webb, a collier, who lived there with his wife, Mary Anne and their six children. Other occupants of the houses included a farm bailiff – a reminder that farming still played a part in the local economy – and a 'sad iron moulder' who probably worked at the nearby iron foundry in Woodsetton.

Top left: *Kitchen of Number 11*

Centre left: *The Brew House in the back yard*

Centre right: *The Back-to Backs, on the left Number 10 and Number 12 on the right divided by the through tunnel*

Right: *the kitchen of Number 12*

All three houses have the usual cast-iron open fire kitchen ranges with an oven although the kitchen of Number 12 also contains an early cast-iron gas cooker. Number 12 is lit with an incandescent gas light whilst in 10 and 11 a meagre light is provided by a single gas bracket lamp fitted with a fish tail burner, named after the shape of the flame. These simple gas lights, dating from the 1820s, remained universal until the advent of the incandescent gas light after 1893.

The privy in the yard of Number 11 has been rebuilt with a stoneware tipper closet which was patented in 1887 by James Duckett of Burnley. As these toilets were flushed only intermittently by an underground tipper tank which collected waste water, they were liable to become dirty and smelly unless lots of extra water was poured in from the top by the householder; this one came from Toll End, Tipton.

Chapel Street, Halesowen

Nail Shop

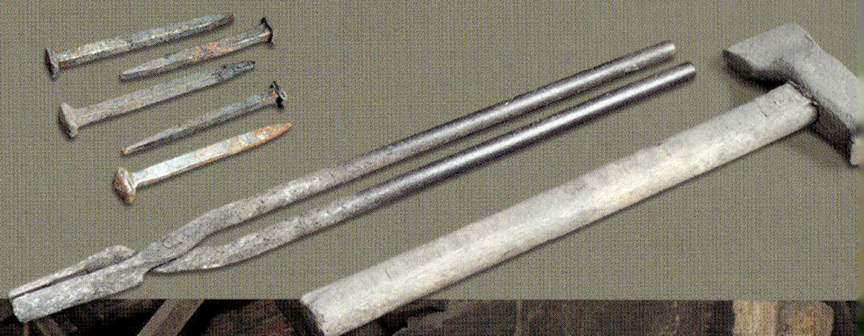

The contents of the Nail Shop were taken from a workshop located behind 17 Chapel Street, Halesowen dating to the 1880s and last operated by Sidney Tether in the 1940s. The structure is a replica of the original building.

The hand making of nails is one of the oldest specialist iron trades of the Black Country: Dudley was famed for its nails in the sixteenth century. The industry reached its peak in c. 1830 when there were 50,000 nail makers at work in the region, principally around Dudley, Sedgley, Gornal, Lye, Halesowen and Old Hill. From the 1830s there was a sharp decline in the trade due to the introduction of machine made nails and by 1865 numbers of hand nail makers had fallen to 20,000. The trade remained strongest in the south and west of the Black Country although there were pockets of the industry in Bromsgrove and elsewhere outside the region. By 1881 only a small proportion of nails of specialist type were still hand wrought in the Dudley area. The last hand nailer retired in about 1952 in the Bromsgrove area.

Nail makers worked for nail masters or 'foggers' who supplied them with the nail rod iron or as outworkers for large firms such as Eliza Tinsley who from 1853, operated large works at Old Hill producing wrought-iron nails, rivets, chains, chain cables and anchors. The making of nails was carried out typically in small work shops attached to or close to the nailer's home. This nail shop has shuttered unglazed windows for ventilation and originally contained two hearths, each worked by two nailers. The hearths are placed centrally as in most nail shops as this allowed several members of the family to work around it. The nails were pointed, cut to size and headed on a strike block using an over-hammer or 'oliver' with an interchangeable die stamp. The hammer is held up by a wooden spring pole and brought down on the hot metal by a foot operated lever.
As the trade declined two of the olivers were removed and replaced by an anvil so that the general forging of oddwork, such as hooks and brackets, could be done.

Above: *The nail shop originally stood in the back yard of a house in Chapel Street, Halesowen*

Top: *The interior of the nail shop with the Museum's nail maker framed by the sprung pole of the oliver.*

60 *setting:* **c.1900**

Shaw Street, Walsall

Brass Foundry

The Brass Foundry was built in Shaw Street, Walsall for Henry Crowther and dates to 1869 when there were some 500 men employed in brass casting in the town.

Brass is an alloy of copper and zinc. It was made into a vast range of finished goods by braziers who worked the metal in sheet form or by brass founders who cast objects by pouring molten brass into moulds. Brass foundries were established in Birmingham and elsewhere in the West Midlands in the 1690s and by the nineteenth century, Birmingham was established as the capital of brass production with many founders specialising in particular products, such as cabinet brassware, cocks and taps and candlesticks. In Walsall brass founders specialised in brassware for the harness trade including stirrups and horse brasses which reached their peak of popularity in the late nineteenth century.

The foundry originally made small items of horse harness such as stirrups, bits, buckles and hames in both iron and brass. Horse brasses were also made and over 200 patterns made of lead for different designs of horse brass can be seen on the wall along with patterns for stirrups and pot hooks. The pattern is the master copy and the quality of the pattern, as in all casting work, determines the quality of the finished article. Equally, careful preparation of the mould is vital to a successful casting. The brass founder makes the mould by pressing special moulding sand around the pattern in a rectangular frame made in two halves so that the pattern can be easily removed leaving a cavity. The sand is kept in a large wooden trough - or tub - under one of the windows. Meanwhile the brass – usually consisting of scrap metal – is melted in a fireclay crucible placed in a coke fired furnace until the brass reaches its melting point of 900-940 degrees centigrade. Using long handled tongs, the founder lifts the crucible of molten metal and carefully pours it into a hole in the side of the mould called a 'runner'. When the metal has cooled the mould is broken away to remove the new casting which is then finished to remove all roughness using a lathe, file or polishing machine.

The foundry closed at the end of the Second World War and lay unused for 20 years but it was returned to use by James Powell in 1964 for the making of hames and other items of horse harness in non-ferrous metals such as aluminium bronze. The foundry was finally closed in 1973 when James Powell died and the building and equipment was carefully taken in 1986 for rebuilding at the Museum.

Top: *Withdrawing the crucible from the furnace with long handled tongs*

Middle: *The moulds into which the hot metal is poured are formed in the sand tub under the window*

Right: *The foundry seen from the tunnel or gunnel of the Back-to-backs*

61 *setting:* c.1900

Birmingham Street, Oldbury

The Bakery

The coal fired Bakery from Oldbury is representative of the small independent bakeries which were once a common part of every Victorian and early twentieth century town in the Black Country and across Britain. In Wednesbury, for example, there were 31 bake houses with their own shops in the 1920s and for each of them the sale of bread and confectionery through delivery rounds was an important part of the business.

The building probably dates to c. 1845. In 1844 the site of the bakery was purchased by Thomas Millership, a coal miner; he mortgaged the land and built on it. When he sold it in 1849 one of the occupiers, Benjamin Roden, was described as a confectioner. This is the earliest evidence of baking on the premises. In 1879 the property was auctioned as five lots including two dwelling houses and shops (later 48 and 50 Birmingham Street), together with the bakehouse and outbuildings which were situated between the back of the two shops and a flour mill. The buyer was George Veal who was already the tenant and so through this purchase he became the owner of both the bakery and the baker's shop 46 fronting the street.

The bakery continued in business until 1952 when the last baker, Samuel Harvey, retired. Thereafter the premises were used for storage and fell into disrepair. When the Museum rescued the building in 1977 it was entirely derelict with virtually no roof remaining. The Museum rebuilt it brick by brick and completed the interior with fittings from Clarke's bakery in Mount Pleasant, Bilston. Every day bread is baked in the coal fired cast-iron oven as it was recalling a way of life that has disappeared.

62 Chain Making Shop (*setting:* c.1900)

The Chain Shop is not a reconstruction or replica of any original building but is typical of many Black Country chain shops. The hearths are copies of two from Noah Bloomer's works in Quarry Bank with a third, a replica of one from Cradley Heath.

The making of heavy chains and cables in the Black Country was introduced in c. 1824 and made in large works such as Noah Hingley's of Netherton. Smaller chain was made in workshops like this one or by outworkers in small back yard chain shops. By the mid-nineteenth century, much of the Britain's chain production was centred on Cradley and Cradley Heath, Quarry Bank, Netherton and Old Hill. The making of handmade wrought-iron chain declined in the face of electrically welded steel cable chain from the 1930s and finally came to an end during the winter of 1976-77 when supplies of wrought-iron finally dried up.

The process of chain making consists of heating pre-cut rods of iron in the fire and bending the rod to a U Shape on the anvil with blows from the chainmaker's hammer. The U is then reheated in the fire, removed and threaded through the end link on the end of chain and the ends flattened and wrapped around each other. The link is then reheated and welded together, reheated again and finished into shape with the tommy hammer.

The fuel for the chain makers' hearths is 'breeze', a small size of coke. Coke is simply coal that had been burned in a closed chamber to burn off the volatile ingredients supplying a smokeless fuel that provides the smith with a clear, hot fire.

63 Blacksmith's Shop (*setting:* c.1900)

The Blacksmith's Shop is housed in a reconstructed building from Great Bridge which retains its original corner fireplace. The equipment is from Eliza Tinsley's Works in Old Hill.

Above right: *The Bakery has been rebuilt in a back yard behind the Cake Shop in keeping with its former location in Birmingham Street, Oldbury*

Bottom: *Shutting (or welding) the link at the Chain Shop forge*

Birchley Works, Oldbury

Rolling Mill

The Rolling Mill was installed at Birchley Works, Oldbury, in 1923 and ceased work in 1976 when it was relocated at the Museum occupying a typical canal side location which in its working life would have enabled the easy movement by canal boat of the raw materials and finished products.

Before wrought-iron could be used by specialist iron workers it had to be converted into sheet metal or cut into bars which were either made flat or profiled for particular uses. The earliest type of rolling mill was the slitting mill which was adopted in the Black Country in the seventeenth century to cut or slit iron to a fixed width and this flat bar was used for the rims of wagon wheels and the hoops of barrels. Slitting mills were also used to produce the thin rods of iron which were required by the many nailers of the region. The Rolling Mill was developed from the slitting mill in the eighteenth century and became an integral part of the typical large Black Country ironworks.

In the rolling mill, lengths of wrought-iron or mild steel are heated in the furnace connected to the 45 feet high brick chimney; originally coal fired, the furnace is now equipped with two oil burners. When the bars have reached a temperature of about 1200°C and are 'margarine coloured' they are pulled out of the furnace and passed through a series of shaped rollers held in stands to reduce the size or shape in section. The gaps between the rollers are arranged to be progressively smaller, each pass slowly reducing the thickness until the final size is achieved. A supply of cold water is directed at the rollers and the bearings to ensure they remain hard and cold whilst in contact with the hot metal. The operators stand either side of the roller stands. Passing the red-hot bars of iron into and out of the rollers using long handled tongs required considerable strength and skill.

This particular mill is typical of the period c. 1880-1930 being of a simple open train design with the roll stands in a straight line and drive supplied by an electric motor. At Birchley the Mill produced a wide range of small rounds, squares, hexagons, flats and special sections but was considerably altered over time.

The Museum operates the rolling mill at advertised times through the year with the assistance of a skilled workforce of volunteers experienced in hand rolling.

Top: *Feeding the red hot bars back through the bolting rolls*

Above: *The roll stands in the* ***Rolling Mill***

65 *setting:* **c.1900**

Level Street, Brierley Hill

Ironworker's Office

The Ironworker's Office has been reconstructed out of a simple two up two down cottage from Level Street, Brierley Hill, near Dudley. Little is known about its history but it is believed to date from the early nineteenth century.

When it was discovered by the Museum in 1981 it was semi-derelict but still in use as an office for a welder's yard. It was carefully dismantled in 1982 and rebuilt at the Museum. The building had suffered some subsidence and the resulting irregularities were preserved in the rebuilding. It is presented as the office and mess area of an ironworks. The front office contains samples of rolled iron section and patterns for turning the rods.

66 *built:* **1879 & 1922**

Factory Junction Bridge and Brown's Bridge

At the bottom of the Village the Lifting Bridge connects the street to the Boat Dock, spanning the Museum's Canal Arm near its entrance to the main canal.

The bridge originally crossed the railway transhipment basins of Lloyd's Proving House near Factory Junction at Tipton. The bridge was built by Armstrong & Main of Newcastle upon Tyne in 1922. It has a span of 28 feet and is twelve feet six inches wide. The bridge is lifted manually by operating spur wheels through gearing which lowers the two five ton counterweights suspended by chains from the uprights of the portal frame.

Brown's Bridge crosses the Museum's Canal Arm at its junction with the Dudley Canal and was originally located at the gas works at Swan Village, West Bromwich. It is named in memory of J A Brown, a British Waterways engineer.

Top left: *The 'Dial Time Recorder' clocking-in machine from Charles Rowley & Co., Birmingham, c. early 1900s*

Top right inset: *The Level Street office in its semi-derelict state before the take down*

Centre right: *The Ironworker's Office with a bracket gas lamp on the corner of the building*

Above: *The Factory Junction Lifting Bridge crossing the Museum's Canal Arm with Brown's Bridge behind*

Woods Lane, Cradley Heath

Anchor Forge

Right: *Anchor making at the forge of Samuel Taylor & Sons, Brettel Lane, Brierley Hill (established c. 1879); in the background under the extended roof, the furnace, a steam hammer and two cranes are visible*

The Museum's Anchor Forge is set in the 1920s and preserves the equipment from the last anchor forge to operate in the Black Country. Surprisingly, perhaps, for a region so far from the sea, for over a hundred years, anchor making was one of its most prominent industries and anchors for some of the most famous ships of the nineteenth and twentieth centuries, including Brunel's 'Great Eastern', the 'Titanic' and the Royal Yacht, 'Britannia' were forged in the Black Country.

Following the introduction of the making of heavy chain in the region in the 1820s, Noah Hingley started making anchors at Netherton in 1838. The industry expanded rapidly and by 1868 there were 14 firms making anchors chiefly in Cradley, Netherton and Tipton including James Lane's forge, established in Woods Lane, Cradley Heath, in 1867. In the mid-1920s the business was taken over by Isaiah Preston who supplied anchors to the Royal Navy and the Royal National Lifeboat Institution. In the 1970s the average weekly output was seven tons of a wide range of anchor types but the business closed in the spring of 1979 bringing to an end 140 years of anchor making in the region.

The Museum collected the steam hammer, furnace and chimney base along with the boiler and an old egg-ended boiler used as a water tank. The wrought-iron to be forged was heated in the furnace. 'Waste heat' from the furnace was drawn through the single flue of the large horizontal 'Cornish' boiler which raised steam to power the steam hammer. The furnace was originally coal fired but converted to oil firing in 1969. This boiler is not the original but a near identical one from Walsall. When the pieces of wrought-iron reached welding heat, the mass of metal was removed from the furnace and hammered to the required shape by the steam hammer.

Top: *The steam hammer of c. 1886 framed by the cranes used to lift heavy forgings in the Museum's reconstruction of Isaiah Preston's anchor forge*

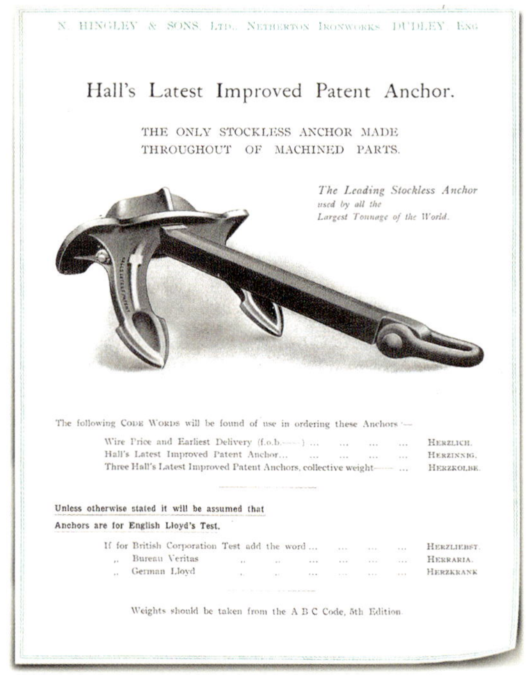

N. HINGLEY & SONS, LTD., NETHERTON IRONWORKS, DUDLEY, ENG.

Hall's Latest Improved Patent Anchor.

THE ONLY STOCKLESS ANCHOR MADE THROUGHOUT OF MACHINED PARTS.

The Leading Stockless Anchor used by all the Largest Tonnage of the World.

The following CODE WORDS will be found of use in ordering these Anchors:—

Wire Price and Earliest Delivery (f.o.b.——)	HERZLICH.
Hall's Latest Improved Patent Anchor...	HERZINNIG.
Three Hall's Latest Improved Patent Anchors, collective weight—— ...	HERZKOLBE.

Unless otherwise stated it will be assumed that Anchors are for English Lloyd's Test.

If for British Corporation Test add the word	HERZLIEBST.
,, Bureau Veritas	HERRARIA.
,, German Lloyd	HERZKRANK

Weights should be taken from the A B C Code, 5th Edition.

Above: *In 1891, Noah Hingley of Netherton agreed rights to manufacture Hall's stockless anchor first patented in 1886; Hingleys supplied many ships with these anchors including the White Star liners, 'Olympic' and 'Titanic'*

James Nasmyth (1808-90) patented the steam hammer in 1842 to forge large pieces of iron more effectively than the traditional tilt hammer. The hammer block – or 'tup' – was connected to the piston of a steam engine; by controlling the passage of the steam to the cylinder it was possible to control the intensity of the blow and its frequency. Using the steam hammer it was now possible to forge anchors in one piece resulting in a much stronger end product. Noah Hingley was the first Black Country maker to use a steam hammer in 1850 and James Lane is known to have installed one by 1877 although this hammer, made by Charles Ross of Sheffield and dating to c. 1886, is thought to have been acquired second hand in c. 1900; its tup gives a one ton blow under gravity.

As only the bottom 16 feet of the chimney survived in 1979, the original full height was restored using bricks from two chimneys in Bloxwich. The building came from Johnson's Rolling Mill, in Hill Top, West Bromwich and with its cast-iron columns and timber roof trusses is a typical late nineteenth century Black Country industrial structure.

The 50 feet high square brick chimney of the Anchor Forge

The massive 16 ton bow anchor of R.M.S. 'Titanic' at Lloyd's Proof House, Netherton, loaded onto a flat bed wagon of the London & North Western Railway to begin the first leg of its journey to Harland & Wolff's ship yard in Belfast, 1 May 1911

68 *from:* 1839

The Boat Dock & Boat Collection

The Museum has built the Boat Dock on a canal branch believed to have been formed by mining subsidence in the middle of the nineteenth century. This branch formerly joined the canal arm built in 1839 to link the Limekilns with the Birmingham Canal Navigations (BCN).

The Black Country is criss-crossed by a dense network of canals belonging to the BCN. From the authorisation of the first canal in the region in 1767 the system expanded rapidly and facilitated the rapid expansion of industry in the region; even the coming of the railways could not diminish the importance of short distance boat transport to local business. Only the expansion of the road network in the mid-1900s finally made canal transport unviable in the Black Country.

Although long distance boats were seen on the BCN, short haul cargoes characterised the traffic on these canals. Many of the Museum's canal boats are these simple open day boats; designed to carry crucial loads of coal, iron, limestone and clay relatively short distances. Often, there was no provision of even basic shelter for the steerers, who could return home after their day's work. The Museum is also home to a very particular type of day boat, the 'joey', which can be steered from either end, removing the need to turn the boat around.

Canal boats were gauged to measure their capacity; this gauging plate was fixed to 'Bessie' when she was regauged in 1916

For most of the BCN's history, wooden horse drawn boats would have been the most common sight. In time, other materials became common in boat construction: iron, composite boats with iron sides and wooden bottoms, and also boats with entirely steel hulls. Steam and motor boats came into use, but in the Black Country horsepower never entirely fell out of favour.

The Museum collection represents a range of construction and boat type. ***Bessie,*** now permanently out of the water, is the oldest boat in the collection, dating to 1895. The youngest boat, ***Birchills*** (built 1953), is also one of the most important, being the last surviving wooden joey boat with a day cabin. There is steam boat ***President*** (1909) with its butty boat ***Kildare*** (1913). Sheltering on the dock, as though being given a new set of wooden bottoms, is composite boat ***Diamond*** (1926). There are also two examples of 'station' boats which worked the canal-rail interchange on behalf of the railway companies. ***Stour*** (1937) is a very fine example of a long distance, wooden built motor boat which was operated for most of its working life by one family.

Work began on the Museum boat dock in 1976, with the aim of creating a careful replica of the docks which were once common on the BCN. It was built traditionally, often from the recycled timbers of derelict wooden boats, as would have been the case on smaller docks. Such docks were principally for the construction of wooden boats or the maintenance of iron and composite boats.

Top left: *'Bessie', a typical Black Country iron day boat built 1895 and originally owned by the Hart's Hill Iron Co., Brierley Hill, and from the 1930s until the 1970s by Stewarts & Lloyds*

There are a number of different buildings here, each with a particular purpose. The brick built blacksmith's shop is of 1880s design. It houses a workbench from the BCN maintenance yard at Icknield Port, Birmingham, a general purpose hearth and hand bellows. The metal work for constructing or repairing boats would be wrought in this shop, from specialised nails and bolts through to the L shaped boat 'knees' used to reinforce the boat structure. Some blacksmiths may even have turned their hand to shoeing boat horses.

Abutting the blacksmith's shop is a series of individual sheds, the front of which is formed from the recycled bottom of a wooden boat; inside the sheds, the boat knees are still visible. There is a nail store then a slightly larger rivet store. The latter includes provision of a carpenter's bench and the comfort of a cast-iron stove made by Tangye of Smethwick. At the end of this row is a small paint store for housing the basic ingredients used on boats: white lead, red lead, pigments and varnishes. The door is coloured by years of brushes rubbed out against the timber.

Beyond these sheds is the tackle store, with its corrugated roof, which would once have housed lifting tackle and other equipment for handling the boats. Alongside is the up-ended stern of an old joey boat, used as a toilet by dock workers. At the opposite end of the dock there is the stable for boat horses, which provided both power to move the boats and also an important element of 'hosmuck an' tar', used to seal wooden boats.

The dock is completed with vital equipment such as a saw shed; the steam chest, for heating planks for bending; two types of side slipway, for bringing boats in and out of the water; and a moveable rolling shed, to provide some protection to workers from the elements. Scattered about are old boat bottoms, boat knees and other odd items which would lie about a dock awaiting recycling in boats or buildings.

Top right page 66: *Steam Boat* ***'President'*** *was built by Fellows, Moreton & Clayton at their Saltley Boat Dock in 1909 and worked 'fly' (day and night) chiefly along the Grand Union Canal between the Midlands and London*

Top: *The Boat Dock with sheds and the privy or toilet made from the stern of an old Joey boat*

Above: *'President' at Buckby on the Grand Union Canal, c. 1911*

Above right: *Mast head lamp from 'Stour' made by Griffiths & Sons Ltd., Birmingham*

setting: c.1905

New Road, Willenhall *(at original location)*

The Locksmith's House

The Locksmith's House of 54 New Road, Willenhall, is typical of the small, family run lock making businesses which once characterised the town. Although locks were also made in nearby Wolverhampton and Walsall, the concentration of skills and domestic workshops in Willenhall gave it a reputation as the lock making centre of Britain. Even in the early 1900s, when the trade had shifted towards larger factories, backyard concerns like this one at New Road continued to survive.

New Road was both home and workplace for the Hodson family, who rented the workshops for a time before buying the entire property in 1904. By this time, the business of 'Richard Hodson & Sons', which claimed to go back as far as 1792, was owned by John Hodson. He brought his wife Sarah with him, along with their son Edgar and their three daughters, Ida, Edith and Flora. When John died, Edgar continued the business of making bar padlocks and lighter locks, and latterly other activities such as stamping out spanners and supplying parts for oven doors.

All the facilities for stamping and forging lock parts, assembling them and finishing them are located behind the house. There is the main two storey workshop; the ground floor where smithing was done, the upper storey where the locks were assembled. The ground floor still contains a hearth, hand bellows, an impressive original floor press, and a number of presses driven by line shafting. Across the yard there was a single storey stamping shop, now converted to an education room, where the lock parts were once stamped out from sheet iron or brass. Behind the kitchen is a small room containing a japanning oven (similar to a fire heated kiln), for 'cooking' the painted surface of locks to finish them.

54 New Road, Willenhall, home to the Hodson family of Locksmiths from 1905 to c. 1970. The goods entrance, leading to the courtyard and workshops is on the right

***Top:** An Edwardian bedroom in the Locksmith's House*

The house itself dates to 1840, but the interiors are displayed as they would have looked in 1905, using much of the family's original furniture and other belongings. The front room contains a changing display of working class clothing and accessories, reflecting the draper's shop set up here in the 1920s by sisters Edith and Flora. It is a selection from their unsold stock which forms the display. Upstairs is the Lock Gallery, with its nationally significant collection of locks and keys. This covers the main developments in lock making from antiquity and all the major British makers - Robert Barron and Joseph Bramah, Chubb, Yale and Josiah Parkes, makers of Union locks - are included. The products of other local manufacturers who have now disappeared are represented in the display including the 'Albert Lock' made by Carpenter & Tildesley for the Great Exhibition in 1851.

Above: *The parlour of the Locksmith's House*

Top Left: *The Albert Lock made for the Great Exhibition of 1851 by Carpenter & Tidlesley of Willenhall; this rim lock contains wards, levers and a Bramah mechanism*

Costumed Characters

Behind shop counters, on the street, in houses, or hammering in workshops, costumed Demonstrators wear period costume to meet visitors every day. Their clothes are central to the Living Museum and a great deal of research goes into getting them right.

When a new building is developed, or an old one is refreshed, an expert group of curators, seamstresses and front of house staff prepare the clothing that its past users would have worn. Winter and summer outfits are prepared, hairstyles considered, and accessories such as tools or umbrellas added.

Sources of information include local photographs and illustrations, written accounts and oral history. Where evidence exists, the team recreates the clothing of real, named people, who lived or worked in buildings in the past. Lilian Hodgkiss, who lived in the Toll House (No.14), worked at the National Projectile Factory in Hall Street, Dudley during the First World War. Curators found photographs of 'munitionettes' working at the factory in Dudley Archives and the Imperial War Museum. Along with written records, these helped the Museum seamstress to design and recreate Lilian's uniform, including her mop cap. For Adey's Greengrocers (No. 49), shop aprons from the early 1900s were researched and recreated in a style that fitted the humble nature of the shop. To dress for the Museum's workshops, photographs of working men at the forges and hammers of the Black Country were consulted to make recreations of working clothes such as leather aprons.

The Museum is always glad to receive photographs of people at work in the past, to strengthen our research archives

Street Furniture

On any older street, there are many features of interest which people usually hurry past. We hardly notice them as we go about our daily lives. They might be very ordinary things such as post boxes, railings, street lamps, signs and even kerbs. Yet these features, known as street furniture, contain many fascinating little histories of their own. They all help to set a scene, or tell the story of a place. For this reason, the Museum seeks to get these details right.

The nineteenth century saw the greatest flourishing of ornate street furniture ever known. The great material that made it possible was cast-iron. As an ironmaking district, the Black Country proudly crafted fine street furniture for use around the world. But it was also a district plagued by poverty and industrial waste that created other 'accidental' forms of street furniture, such as abandoned machinery. The Museum has recreated some of these in the landscape too. We plan to improve and increase the amount of street furniture on show in the years to come and are always glad to hear of items that could be added to our streets.

9 ***Top:*** *Trolleybus stop sign*

37 ***Middle:*** *Cast iron kerbs*

17 ***Bottom:*** *Scrap yard full of items awaiting restoration or use around the Museum*

20 ***Top:*** *Electric lamps along tramway, Magnalite type – popular in the 1930s manufactured by Revo of Tipton*

23 ***Middle:*** *School railings, Bayliss, Jones and Bayliss of Wolverhampton*

6 ***Bottom:*** *Give way sign. Pre-1939*

65 ***Top:*** *Replica flat flame gas lamp using the Camberwell Pattern c.1910*

25 ***Middle:*** *Tar laying machine c.1910*

12 ***Bottom:*** *Early haystack boiler c.1770*

25 ***Top:*** *Gas lamp, Cochrane of Dudley*

33 ***Middle:*** *Drinking fountain c.1912*

5 ***Bottom:*** *Tram pole base, British Electric Traction Co. c.1890-1920*

23 ***Right:*** *Sewer gas lamp school corner. Cast iron column, 'Webb Patent Birmingham'.*

The world's first industrial landscape

Black Country Timeline...

1292 First mention of coal mines at Pensnett

1538 Henry VIII orders nails from Reynold Warde of Dudley for building at Hampton Court

1557 Refugees from Lorraine, France, introduce glass making to Stourbridge

1575 Elizabeth I visits Dudley

1581 First recorded death of a Black Country coal miner, William Price

1621 The Earl of Dudley is granted a patent for the production of iron using pit coal

1665 Dud Dudley (1599-1684) describes his method of using coke for smelting iron in 'Metallum Martis'

1678 Abraham Darby I is born in Wren's Nest, Dudley on 14 April

1701 The Wolverhampton, Dudley & Birmingham Turnpike Trust established

1709 Abraham Darby commences smelting iron with coke at Coalbrookdale, Shropshire

1712 The world's first steam engine invented by Thomas Newcomen and installed at a mine at Coneygree, Tipton

1740 Four blast furnaces producing iron in South Staffordshire and Worcestershire

1749 John Wesley, the founder of Methodism makes his first visit to Dudley

1769 First Black Country canal is constructed, from Wednesbury to Birmingham

1770 Richard Salter makes the first spring balance about this time at Bilston

1775 Lord Dudley & Ward begins building a branch canal from the Birmingham Canal at Tipton into his limestone mines beneath Castle Hill

1776 One of the first two Boulton & Watt condenser engines is installed at a mine in Bloomfield, Tipton to pump water

1779 Dudley & Stourbridge Canal completed

1785 Work begins on extending the Dudley Canal Tunnel by two miles to connect with the Stourbridge Canal at Parkhead

1787 Iron master John Wilkinson issues copper halfpenny tokens bearing his own effigy – the first such coin with a head other than the monarch's

1791 Dudley Canal Tunnel completed

1791 Archibald Kenrick, Ironfounder of West Bromwich sets up business

1792 The Hodson family set up business as lock makers in Willenhall

1796 Soho Foundry, Smethwick opened by Boulton & Watt to manufacture steam engines

1798 Dudley Number 2 Canal opens between Parkhead and Bumble Hole

1800 26 blast furnaces in operation in the Black Country

1802 William Jones establishes the first Black Country brewery in Snow Hill, Wolverhampton

1811 John Russell begins to make wrought-iron tube in Wednesbury

1815 Archibald Kenrick patents the first cast-iron coffee mill

1816 Aaron Manby lights the Horsley Ironworks, Tipton by gas, probably the first use of gas lighting in the Black Country

1817 Sir Humphrey Davy's miners' safety lamp introduced in the Black Country

1821 Wolverhampton becomes the first Black Country town to be lit by gas

1823 84 blast furnaces making iron in the Black Country

1825 Cornelius Whitehouse invents a method of forging hollow tubes

1829 Foster Rastrick & Co. of Stourbridge build 'Agenoria', the first steam locomotive to run in the Midlands and the 'Stourbridge Lion' America's first steam locomotive

1830 James Carpenter of Willenhall and John Young of Wolverhampton patent a lift up rim lock from which the modern mortice lock was developed

1830 The artist J.M.W. Turner visits Dudley and later depicts the town in water colour

1832 Robert Lucas Chance patents 'Improved Cylinder Glass' widely used for larger glass windows

1832 First cholera epidemic sweeps across the Black Country

1834 First recorded use of the name 'The Black Country'.

1835 First fight of William Perry, the 'Tipton Slasher' (1819-80), the champion prize-fighter of England from 1850-57

1835 Construction of the first reservoir in the Black Country is begun at Shavers End by the Dudley Waterworks Company

1837 The first main line railway in the Black Country – the Grand Junction Railway - reaches Wolverhampton

1837 Robert Spear Hudson pioneers the first commercially successful dry soap powder in West Bromwich

1839 Joseph Hall of the Bloomfield Ironworks, Tipton discovers the 'wet puddling' process of making high quality wrought-iron

1841 Joseph Bramah and Alexander Brodie Cochrane build the Woodside Ironworks and Foundry in Dudley

1841 Charles Dickens includes a powerful description of the Black Country in 'The Old Curiosity Shop'

1842 The Earl of Dudley's massive new limekilns (now part of the Black Country Living Museum) become operational

1848 Noah Hingley establishes commercial production of chains and anchors in the Black Country

1849 Francis T. Rufford of Stourbridge makes the first one-piece fireclay bath

1849 Second major cholera epidemic

1850 First batch of iron columns for the Crystal Palace are delivered from Cochrane's Woodside Foundry, Dudley

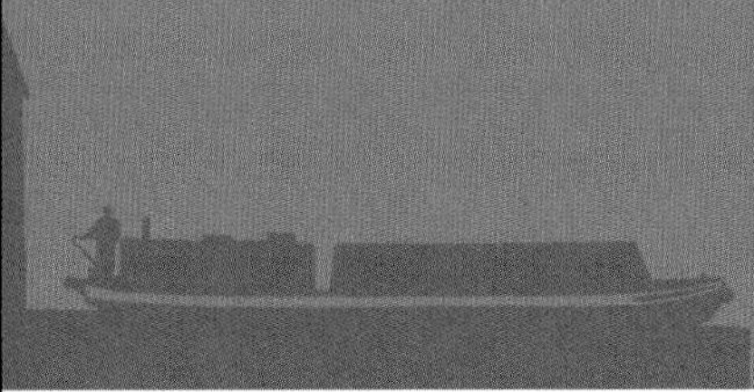

1850 First steam hammer in the Black Country is installed by James Nasmyth at Noah Hingley's Netherton works

1851 Chance Brothers of Smethwick supply the glass for the Crystal Palace in London

1852 Peter Wright of Dudley patents a new anvil which becomes one of the world's finest

1853 Annual death total of Black Country miners peaks at 190

1854 The Oxford, Worcester and Wolverhampton Railway, also known as the 'Old Worse and Worse', reaches Wolverhampton Low Level Station

1856 Arthur Albright and John Edward Wilson form Albright & Wilson the leading suppliers of white and red phosphorous to the match industry

1857 The peak of Black Country iron production with between 120 and 130 blast furnaces producing 777,000 tons of iron

1859 Britain's first standard design of letter box is made by Cochrane's Woodside Foundry in Dudley

1866 Queen Victoria visits Wolverhampton. She reputedly has the windows of her railway carriage closed to hide the view

1868 Alfred Preedy opens his first tobacconist's shop in Dudley

1868 Elihu Burritt the American consul in Birmingham, famously describes the Black Country as, 'Black by Day, Red by Night'

1872 Black Country coal production peaks at 10,550,000 tons per year

1876 The Wolverhampton – Dudley Turnpike Trust is wound up

1878 West Bromwich Albion Football Club formed by workers from Salter's Spring Works

1878 The first horse drawn tramway in the Black Country commences service in Wolverhampton on 1 May

1879 Wolverhampton Wanderers formed by the merger of two clubs, St Luke's and The Wanderers

1883 Steam trams start operation in Dudley

1884 Thomas Parker becomes the first Black Country motorist when he travels to and from work in an electrically powered vehicle of his own design

1888 Walsall Football Club founded as Walsall Town Swifts

1895 W & T Avery Ltd takes over the Soho Foundry in Smethwick

1896 Henry Palethorpe opens a sausage factory in Tipton, reputedly the largest in the world at the time

1897 Henry Doulton begins the manufacture of fireclay goods at Rowley Regis

1899 Construction of Baggeridge Colliery's first shaft begins

1899 Edward Lisle makes the first Star motor car in Wolverhampton

1900 Electric tram service from Dudley to Stourbridge commences

1905 Sunbeam Motor Car Company established in Wolverhampton

1909 Steam boat 'President' is built by Fellows, Moreton & Clayton

1910 The women chain makers of Cradley successfully strike for the first ever minimum wage

1910 The first AJS motor cycle

1911 The massive centre anchor for 'Titanic' is made in Netherton and Halesowen

1913 Workers strike for higher minimum wages in the 'Great Black Country Strike' in April

1914 Commencement of motor bus operation in West Bromwich

1914 Sydney Guy sets up business in Wolverhampton manufacturing commercial vehicles

1915 Zeppelin attack on Dudley in January

1916 Zeppelin raids on Tipton and Wednesbury in January

1919 First Bean automobile runs off the line

1919 V.A. Crabtree & Co. founded in Walsall as electric switch makers

1920 Sunbeam win a record breaking victory at the Isle of Man TT with a top speed of 59.7 MPH

1923 The first trolley bus service in Wolverhampton

1925 Britain's first council house made of cast-iron panels is built in Dudley

1925 Ever Ready move into Wolverhampton

1926 The Limekilns on the Earl of Dudley's Estate close

1927 Wolverhampton – Birmingham New Road opened by Prince of Wales on 2 November

1927 A new land speed record of over 200 mph is set by Henry Segrave driving a 1,000 hp Sunbeam on Daytonna Beach, USA

1939 The last Black Country tram service, between Dudley and Birmingham via Oldbury, closes

1941 Accles & Pollock of Oldbury start production of the sten gun

1942 Ever Ready begin production of radios in Wolverhampton

1959 Frisky Cars of Wolverhampton introduce the 'Family Three', a three wheeled small saloon car

1962 Last steam train service from Wolverhampton to Stourbridge Junction via Dudley

1962 Dudley Canal Tunnel abandoned by the British Transport Commission and both portals sealed off

1964 Stafford Road Railway works, Wolverhampton, once the workshop of the northern division of the Great Western Railway, closes

1967 The Black Country Society formed

1968 Baggeridge Colliery, the last Black Country coal mine closes

1970 The last Black Country trolley bus runs in Walsall in October

1973 Lucy Woodhall, the last female chain maker retires in December

1978 **The Black Country Living Museum opens**

1979 The anchor forge of Isaiah Preston, the last in the Black Country, closes

1980 The blast furnace 'Elisabeth' is demolished ending 200 years of iron and steel production in Bilston

1982 Round Oak steelworks closes

1982 Closure of the last hand steel rolling mill in the Black Country

1991 Batham's Best Bitter is voted winner in the best bitter category of the Great British Beer Festival

2009 The Ordnance Survey gives formal recognition to the Black Country in the 'Landranger' map series

2013 On 3 October Linda Connor from East Sussex becomes the eight-millionth visitor to the Black Country Living Museum

Black Country Living Museum

Site Plan

The Museum occupies 26 acres of historically significant shops, homes and workshops.

Orange Numbers

This map refers back to the index numbers on the pages of this Guide to help the reader navigate around the Museum.

Grey Numbers

Some of the items on the map are not included in the descriptions within this Guide.

For up to date information on these items please visit our website.

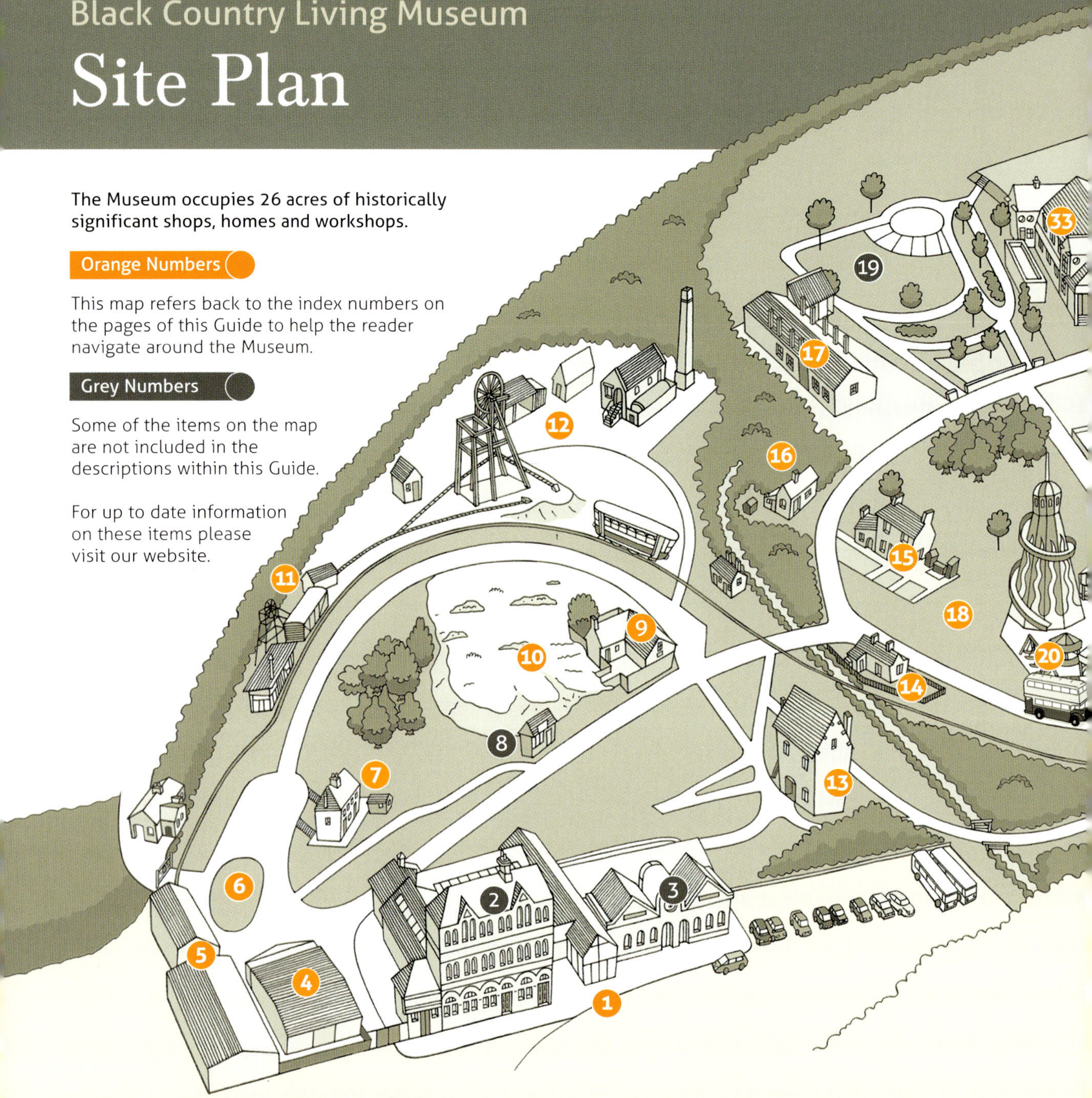

Credits & Acknowledgements

Text by David J Eveleigh

ISBN 978-0-9562031-2-0

The text for the sections, The Boat Dock and the Boat Collection and the Locksmith's House were supplied by **Jo Moody**. Thanks go to **Geoff Cherrington, Trevor Davis, Anthony George, Mike Hessey, Matthew Jones, Stan Letts, Jeff Luesley, David McDougall, Bev Parker, George Price, Brian Rollings, Vic Smallshire, Ian Walden, Clare Weston** and **Irene De Boo.**

Picture credits are as follows: **Andrew Adey,** page 47, **Dudley Archive Service,** page 41 (bottom right); **Dudley Canal Trust,** page 51 (top, centre right and bottom); **Science Museum,** page 17 (bottom); **Staffordshire Record Office,** page 4 (top); **Mike Hessey,** pages 10, 11 (centre left), 24, 25 (bottom), 34 (top), 68 (top); **A R King,** page 36; **Doreen Lowe,** page 28; **David Cave,** page 71 (Woman Chainmaker); **David Martyn,** pages 7 (top), 11 (centre right), 12 (top), 16 (bottom left), 19 (centre right), 22 (top), 27 (bottom right), 37 (bottom), 38 (bottom right), 42 (top right), 44 (top), 47 (top right), 48 (top left), 56 (bottom right), 61 (bottom left), 64 (top), 66 (top left); **Nick Meers,** pages 6 (top), 22 (bottom), 67 (top); **Patrick Mulvaney,** 30 (bottom left), 31 (bottom right), 42 (bottom right); **Stephen Preedy,** page 30; **Ian Stroud,** pages 2-3, 6 (bottom), 8 (bottom), 9 (centre left), 13 (top and bottom), 26 (top), 28 (bottom), 31 (top), 33 (centre left), 37 (top right), 39 (top right), 43 (centre), 46 (bottom), 47 (top), 48 (bottom right), 50 (top), 52 (bottom left), 53 (top), 55 (top), 56 (bottom left), 57 (top left), 59 (centre), 61 (bottom), 63 (bottom), 68 (bottom right), 70 (Sweep, Soldiers & Policeman), 71 (Doctor & Canal Workers); **Selwyn Owens,** the drawing of Rolfe Street Baths on page 7.

First published in Great Britain in 2012 by Black Country Living Museum Publications, a division of Black Country Living Museum Enterprises Ltd, Tipton Road, Dudley, DY1 4SQ, United Kingdom
www. bclm.com
email: info@bclm.com

Designed and produced by Charles Design & Marketing (Kingswinford)

Front cover image:
The Village, Black Country Living Museum (photograph by Nick Meers)
Back Cover: Items from the Museum's collections